## Round 'em up!
## Move 'em out!

Jessie looked first to Ki, and then past the samurai to the cowboys who had been chosen for this drive. Selected from an outstanding crew, these men were the elite, and they knew it. But it worried Jessie that they were already dust-coated and weary-looking, even before the ordeal began. It was the damned punishing heat. Jessie steeled herself, then pulled off her own battered Stetson and waved it in a circle overhead. The cowboys straightened in their saddles and slowly began to drift in behind the herd and set it into motion. They were going to water the herd at the last reservoir on the western boundary of Circle Star; after that they would be taking their chances until they reached the Pecos River.

"Let's move 'em out!" she shouted. "Let's go find ourselves a new cattle market in New Mexico Territory!"

→ **WESLEY ELLIS** ←

# LONE STAR

## AND THE COMANCHEROS

**J**

**JOVE BOOKS, NEW YORK**

# LONE STAR AND THE COMANCHEROS

A Jove book/published by arrangement with
the author

**PRINTING HISTORY**
Jove edition/May 1988

ISBN: 0-515-09549-4

# Chapter 1

Jessica Starbuck stood in her ranch yard and faced a rising sun that burst off the flat Texas horizon. Behind her stood the magnificent Circle Star ranch headquarters, a rambling and very impressive three-storied house, which her father had built using a part of his vast fortune. The late Alex Starbuck had created a worldwide empire which had included shipping, railroads, diamond mines and plantations, but he had loved this great ranch above all the many other homes he had owned around the world. Because that love mirrored her own, Jessie knew she had to save Circle Star.

She took a deep breath and studied her men. They were the best cowboys who could be found in southwest Texas, and there wasn't one among them who could not be counted upon in the face of trouble. They were young, though Ed Wright, her tall, rangy foreman, was in his forties. Their faces were lean and browned by the merciless sun, and there were deep squint lines radiating from the corners of their eyes. *They look punished,* Jessie thought. *Punished by this terrible drought.*

"Men," she said, in a quiet voice that was surprisingly husky for a woman of her uncommon beauty, "I guess we all know why we've gathered here early this morning. For

1

two months, we've all been working from dawn to late at night hauling water and supplemental feed for our herds. So far, we've been able to keep the stock alive and in decent enough shape. I've bought all the hay and grain we could purchase from as far away as Colorado. But this drought has stretched its way out of Texas, and there's no more feed to be bought anywhere."

Jessie glanced over at Ki, her half Japanese, half Caucasian samurai. Ki was both her friend and her protector. She relied on his strength and his wisdom, and had discussed with him this final and desperate act to save what yet remained of her herds. Ed Wright was also in agreement, and there was no better cattleman in Texas. Jessie continued. "Ed and I have decided that we can't afford to wait until this drought ends. We have to assume that there might not be any more rain for months. With the water and grass we have left, we can carry about eight thousand head of cattle almost indefinitely, but that means we'll still have to market about five thousand."

A gust of hot wind whipped across the ranchyard, raising dust and chasing tumbleweeds. Grit stung Jessie's wide, green eyes and she sleeved tears away. She was tall for a woman, narrow-waisted, with high, firm breasts. The rising sun brought out a copper color in her honey-blond hair. She wore tight-fitting denim jeans that accentuated her long legs, and yet the gunbelt around her hip and the leather riding gloves she wore made it plain that she was a woman who rode and worked side by side with her men. Oh, there were better ropers and bronc busters on her payroll, but Jessie had been taught how to make a hand, and if a wild longhorn broke from the herd and caught a cowboy afoot, she could use either a reata or a rifle well enough to save his life.

"Miss Starbuck," a cowboy said, "I reckon you know that most every cattle rancher in Texas is thinkin' along these same lines. I heard tell that the Kansas railheads are jammed with starvin' cattle waitin' to be shipped East. They say that up at Abilene cattle are thicker'n locusts. You can't hardly give 'em away, ma'am."

"We know that," Jessie said tightly. "But I thank you for the warning. What you say is true. There are so many herds in Kansas that they are bringing less than two dollars a head—if they're still alive when they finally get shipped. And as you all know, it's too late to think about driving them all the way to Wyoming where this drought hasn't taken hold. That doesn't leave us with a lot of choices."

Jessie looked back at her foreman. "Ed, why don't you tell the men what we've decided to do."

Ed Wright nodded. He was a slow-talking but quick-thinking man who lived, breathed and dreamed cattle. His face was as dry and weathered as old wood, and his hands were thick from hard work. He led men by his example. It was said that there could be no higher honor for a cowboy than to work under Ed Wright, and after learning Wright's ways with cattle many a cowboy had either gone into ranching on his own or been hired away to ramrod some other big ranching operation.

"All right," he said as the gathering of cowboys leaned forward. "It's about like Miss Starbuck explained. Our options are limited, and none of them are good. But on the other hand, because we've put in a whole lot of earthen reservoirs and taken care never to overgraze this ranch, we aren't in half as bad a shape as most of our neighbors. Still, like them, we're up against some tough choices." Ed studied them closely. "Boys, Miss Starbuck and I have decided that we ought to try driving the five thousand cattle down to Santa Fe, New Mexico."

Every single one of the cowboys blinked.

Ed gave them a few minutes to digest what he'd just announced. "All right," he drawled, "I know that none of you men were figuring on driving cattle through bad Indian country. And before you say anything, we are aware that the Comanche have been raiding down thataway in large numbers. We also know that we may well run into Comancheros and Mexican bandits. It can't be helped. To go north into Kansas like everybody else would be a bad mistake. We're going to deliver these cattle in Santa Fe and try to sell them to the army post there. If the army don't want them all, there's always freighters and teamsters who'll buy 'em and try to make a profit. They might even drive 'em clear to California or Nevada where they'll fetch top dollar. But their risks sure won't be any higher than our own. Miss Starbuck wanted me to make real sure you understood that—and that any man who don't feel like trail-driving through Indian country can stay here and watch the ranch headquarters and take care of the cattle that stays."

Jessie watched the men's reactions. Most of them liked the dangerous gamble, but a few others quite obviously did not. That was expected, and she bore those who might want to remain on the ranch no ill will, nor did she think the less of them. And for those who wanted to go, it was expected that they would give their lives, if necessary, to deliver her thirsty cattle to Santa Fe.

Jessie placed her hat on her head and watched the sun float up from the scorched Texas landscape. "Men, what we've proposed to do won't be easy. There's a whole lot more to all this than just the money. We're talking about Starbuck cattle. Animals bred for their meat as well as toughness. If a journey like this can be done, we are the ones to do it. My father always said we Texans are too dependent upon the northern railroads and markets. If we can save the herd and prove that cattle can be sent profitably to Santa Fe and beyond, then we'll have won a new market that might serve us for years. As it stands now, the Kansas cattle buyers pretty much have things their own

4

way. In hard times like this they've got us by the throat, and they're strangling out a lot of good ranchers with their greed. Ed, Ki and I figure we can change that situation, and there is no better time to try than now, while we're in this terrible drought. I sent a letter to Santa Fe more than a month ago, and the reply just came back. They have plenty of grass and water in those mountains, and they are paying top dollar for good cattle. We can deliver these, spend a month while the cattle fatten up again and then sell them for an honest profit."

One cowboy spoke up. "There's bound to be some terrible stretches between here and Santa Fe. How we gonna find enough feed and water?"

Jessie pointed to the wagons. "We'll use those same freight wagons to haul feed and water as we have been using all along. We'll go straight across the Llano Estacado and then head for the Pecos River. Once we reach it, we can follow it right up into Santa Fe."

"What about the Comancheros?" a cowboy asked. "I hear they're even bloodier than the Indians themselves."

"Not the Apache, they ain't," a cowboy drawled.

Jessie frowned. "We'll just have to face that problem as it comes the same as all the rest we're bound to run into. I also worry about Comancheros. They and the Comanche rule that country, but we've no choice but to face and fight them if necessary to protect our herd."

Jessie took a deep breath. "Men, we're battling for our very existence. As you know, I have my father's inherited business interests that allow me to write off losses, but, as with every other Starbuck enterprise, I am committed to operating this ranch profitably. I can't ask others to sacrifice during hard times and to take risks if I'm not willing to do the same. Besides, we have put our blood and our sweat into our stock. We're going to save them or go down trying."

5

The cowboys nodded their heads vigorously. They liked and understood that kind of talk. Cowboying was a matter of pride. You either took it seriously, or you got the hell off a horse and did something else that was probably a whole lot easier, safer and better paying. But there was nothing half-assed about cowboying under Ed Wright and the Circle Star Ranch. Jessie Starbuck paid her hands the best money in Texas, and she treated her men fairly, from the lowest stableboy right up to Ed Wright himself. Treated them as equals deserving respect.

"When do we leave?"

Jessie nodded to her foreman.

Ed jammed his big hands into his pockets and spat tobacco into the dust. "The cattle are most all gathered already. I reckon we leave day after tomorrow," he said. "That is, if you men will ever uproot yourselves and get to bringing them into headquarters for the gathering."

The cowboys didn't need to be asked twice. With the sun already hot, and heat waves undulating off the barren landscape, they swung into their saddles and galloped away. To someone who did not know better they would have looked unorganized, like a bunch of quail bursting out of the brush, heading randomly in every direction. But that wasn't the case at all. Every cowboy on the payroll had a responsibility for a specific part of the ranch. Upon their several thousand acres, they knew which cattle were weak, which still strong. They would pick out the best for the long traildrive. They'd pick out five thousand of the toughest animals to be found anywhere in the Southwest.

The cowboys knew that a fair part of the success of this bold gamble depended on luck. The Llano Estacado was so vast that even a big herd like the one they'd be trailing might make it through safe and unseen. But more likely their success or failure would depend on tough men, horses and longhorns.

6

Jessie watched her cowboys ride away until they were nothing but tiny dots on the horizon. She sighed and turned to her friend Ki. "I would rather lose the entire herd than even one cowboy."

The samurai nodded. "That's interesting, because there isn't one whose honor would allow you to lose a single unnecessary cow before he risked his life."

"I know."

Ed Wright stepped into his saddle. "I've told the men here to load the wagons and check to make sure all the equipment, the harness and the animals are fit for the drive. With any luck at all, we'll be breathing in the scent of pines within a month or so, where there will be grass aplenty."

Jessie nodded. "We'll get through this all right. But you're going to have to leave part of the crew here to look after all the cattle we don't take. We need at least ten here, Ed."

The foreman frowned. "That's going to make us pretty short-handed, Miss Starbuck. Maybe I should see if I can scare up some more cowboys."

Jessie believed in letting her key managers make the decisions they were paid to make unless she disagreed strongly. "Do you think that's what we ought to do? Bring strangers on a tough drive?"

"No," Ed said after a long pause and a shake of his head, "I guess I don't at that. A drive like this is going to be mighty hard. I'd rather go short than bring in men that I don't completely trust in a tight spot."

"I'll leave that up to you," Jessie said. "I've a great deal of paperwork to attend to before we leave. When I'm done, I'll be out to help you gather cattle."

Ed removed his Stetson and sleeved his forehead of perspiration. "I'll bet it'll be over a hundred degrees in the shade again today. A cool mountain breeze sure will feel good to this old man."

Jessie laughed. "You aren't old, Ed. Now and then, you just *talk* old. There's a big difference."

The ranch foreman put his Stetson back on his thinning pate. "Since your father died here on Circle Star, I worry about you sometimes, Jessie."

"Worry about my cattle," she told him in a gentle voice. "Ki is already my full-time worrier. Isn't that right?"

The samurai looked at her. He didn't need to answer. Everyone who had ever had anything to do with the Starbuck empire knew that it was true.

Jessie and Ki walked into the Starbuck headquarters. The huge front room with its floor-to-ceiling rock fireplace was cool and dim. Even by late afternoon it would be a pleasant sanctuary from the brutal heat outside. On the walls were hunting trophies, and on the floor before the fireplace was a bearskin rug. The furniture was massive, befitting the huge proportions of the house and the man who had built it.

After her father's death, Jessie had made no attempt to feminize the ranch headquarters, though her own bedroom left no doubt that it was occupied by a woman who loved delicate beauty even in the midst of a hard, merciless land.

Jessie walked over to her father's desk and stared at the pile of correspondence from around the world and the ever-present financial reports that she, like Alex, insisted on overseeing personally each month. During a three month period each year, she traveled to every one of her far-flung operations just to oversee that everything was in good order. It almost always was. The men she hired to manage her businesses were the best that money could buy, and she gave them a good deal of autonomy. If they produced and made profits, she rewarded them, as well as the employees, but if they failed she let them go. Alex had not been a perfectionist or even particularly demanding. He had just insisted on honest work for honest pay. He had rewarded success and punished failure, both in himself and the men he hired. Jessie felt the same. To reward mediocrity or condone failure was to encourage it to flourish. Too many people depended on the success of the Starbuck empire to allow any slippage.

"Look at this, Ki! It will take me until the very last minute we leave to finish all this paperwork."

The samurai was unsympathetic. "You could sell just ten percent of your father's empire and still have more cash than anyone in Texas. You could hire a dozen accountants and fifty clerks with the profits from any one of your operations. But you enjoy everything you do."

"Is that what you think?"

"It is what I *know*," the samurai said with great assurance.

Jessie frowned. "Well, right now what I think I ought to do is be out on the range helping the men."

"Then do it."

"I can't. I've got a small matter of another revolution in Peru that threatens my copper mine. And in New Guinea..."

The samurai smiled, only half listening. He remembered how Mr. Starbuck had also hated details and yet forced himself to attend to them personally. Like him, Jessie could not let anything go past her attention.

"I will begin to prepare myself for our journey," Ki said, excusing himself.

Jessie nodded. "I suppose you will meditate and fast? No food?"

"Only for the mind. And then there are the exercises and necessary practice."

"Of course." Jessie understood perfectly. Ki was a martial-arts master, a true samurai. To him, the mental was

9

every bit as important as the physical. He would practice with his weapons, but he would spend even more time refining the sharpest edges of his mind. Hunger helped him do so. "I will tell the cook that you will not be eating with me the remainder of our stay."

"Thank you," Ki said, bowing slightly as he removed himself from the room. Had the thought entered his mind that he was disappointing Jessie by his absence, he would have cut his ears off before making his request. But Jessie understood. She was one of the few women he had ever known who could understand. And besides, they had worked together so well for so long that they could almost read each other's thoughts. Ki loved the beautiful young woman, but only as a man loves a thing that he can never conceive of having. He was devoted to Jessie, and had pledged his life to her protection—as a samurai to his master. Jessie, being often too adventuresome, was not an easy woman to protect. She had many enemies and feared nothing, which sometimes made her less than prudent concerning her own safety.

*Yes,* Ki thought as he moved to his own room and prepared himself to practice with his bow and arrows, *Jessie Starbuck is a woman worthy of self-sacrifice, and she is just bold enough to make my duty challenging—bold and courageous, without being vain or foolish.*

Ki picked up his bow, and his fingers inspected every inch of it carefully. The bow was unlike anything Western man or the American Indian had seen before. It was light-colored, composed of layers of fire-tempered bamboo wood glued together, and bound with red silken thread. It had been made for a samurai by a great craftsman in Japan, and it had belonged to the venerable Hirata, who had taught Ki *kakuto bugei,* "the true samurai's way." The bow possessed an incredible flexibility, and a lightness and strength unsurpassed by anything of its nature in the world.

It could fire an arrow a hundred yards so swiftly that it had no match except for a bullet. Its tips were razor-sharp and would serve as a spear, while its gut string was so superbly wrapped that it could saw through flesh or even wood.

The samurai strung the bow, but even for him it was not easy. Ki was not powerfully built, and yet his smooth muscles were as perfectly formed and suited to action as were those of a mountain lion. Hirata had explained that brute strength was not a real virtue; that a quick man would always kill a slow one and that leverage and skill would overcome a weight or strength advantage. Ki had found this to be true over and over again.

When the bow was strung he inspected his *ebira* quiver, which was lacquered and contained fifteen arrows of varying types, each lethal, each designed for a different purpose. For example, there were "chewers," arrows with corkscrew heads. They were designed to chew into the midsection of an enemy and leave him screaming for the mercy of death. The "cleaver" arrow had a crescent-shaped wafer of steel for a head, and was made to sever ropes or a harness. In Japan, such arrowheads were often used to cut down the flag of an enemy, thus draining his spirit and resolve. The "Death Song" arrow was fitted with a small ceramic head. When unleashed, air whistled through a hole and the arrow actually screamed a death song. Few could stand up to Death Song. And when it struck flesh, the ceramic exploded and the song ended a man's life. When using *inagashi,* which was the style of archery in which the bowman sustained a rapid rate of fire, Ki could fire his bow and special arrows almost as fast as most men could lever and fire a Winchester rifle.

Ki studied his collection of *shuriken* star-blades. They were sharp enough to shave with, and he was never without one; even as he was never without his *tanto* knife, with its long, thin blade of the finest steel. He would not be

11

taking the great *katana*, or ceremonial sword, which was the badge of honor that linked a samurai to his noble ancestors. Ki remembered the days when he had been a student of Hirata. This sword had belonged to the old *ronin*, the masterless samurai. Hirata had prized it above all his other weapons, and had explained that a samurai's sacred sword was so honored that if an unworthy even touched its blade he would be slain without warning. Ki loved the *katana*, but he had to admit that he would never slay any man just for ignorantly touching its blade. Besides, in America the long, ornate *katana* always attracted a great deal of attention. Ki was not a man who liked attention; he was quiet, introspective and serene. He preferred to instruct and enlighten others who failed to behave themselves and gave insult. But if they refused to be enlightened and continued to annoy, Ki had many, many ways to change their unfortunate behavior.

Ki collected his weapons and left his spare room. He would go into the hills until it was time to leave for Santa Fe. He would practice his martial arts and prepare himself mentally for the challenge that he and Jessica Starbuck had chosen to undertake. Something inside told him that this long, desperate traildrive was to be dangerous and filled with trials. His inner senses warned the samurai that death awaited many of the Starbuck men, and perhaps even Jessica herself, if he were not perfectly prepared.

The samurai did not go to the barn for his horse. In this heat and with so little water, an animal would suffer. But not a samurai. Pain was only a state of mind that could distort, even obscure, serenity and focus. Ki would not feel the heat or suffer from lack of food. And on the day after tomorrow when the roundup began, he would be ready.

# Chapter 2

They were ready. Jessie stood up in her stirrups and surveyed the huge herd of thirsty cattle. The five thousand head of Texas longhorns were bawling and stomping the dust, already irritable from being gathered for this hard journey. They would not want to leave Circle Star and would have to be driven hard for the first few days. Jessie knew as well as the cowboys that longhorn cattle were territorial creatures, and it was not uncommon for those who escaped a traildrive to walk hundreds of miles back to their home range.

Jessie looked first to Ki, and then past the samurai to the cowboys who had been chosen for this drive. Selected from an outstanding crew, these men were the elite, and they knew it. But it worried Jessie that they were already dust-coated and weary-looking, even before the ordeal began. It was the damned punishing heat. Jessie steeled herself, then pulled off her own battered Stetson and waved it in a circle overhead. The cowboys straightened in their saddles and slowly began to drift in behind the herd and set it into motion. They were going to water the herd at the last reservoir on the western boundary of Circle Star; after that they would be taking their chances until they reached the Pecos River.

"Let's move 'em out!" she shouted. "Let's go find ourselves a new cattle market in New Mexico Territory!"

The cowboys cinched down their hats and pulled their bandannas over the lower half of their lean faces. A huge cloud of dust was immediately kicked up and the drive was underway. Jessie knew it was one that they would not soon forget.

The first few days were hell, just as Ed had predicted and they all had anticipated. The belligerent longhorns kept trying to break from the herd and turn back to the Circle Star. Over and over the cowboys were forced to leave their positions on the drive and chase after some escape-minded cow or steer and rope it. That was when things really got interesting; as thirsty and cranky as the cattle were, roping them made them lower their long, sweeping horns and attack. And when a cowboy had over a thousand pounds of fighting bone, muscle and horn coming straight at him and his horse, it could be an awesome sight, even to a veteran cowboy.

Skill and unerring teamwork were their salvation. As soon as a cowboy saw a friend in that sort of trouble, he was expected to race in and toss another loop over those vicious horns and either "bust" the enraged longhorn by cutting its back legs out from under it, or at least turn the charging animal. If the cowboy missed his loop, it could be disastrous for the first roper.

Fortunately, there were few misses, and when they did occur there was always another Circle Star cowboy sweeping in to make the saving toss. Like her cowboys, Jessie changed horses at least five times each day. The remuda was a busy place. Her own personal mount, Sun, was a tall racing palomino, but no cow-pony. She saved Sun for any emergency that might arise, because the horse was simply too valuable to risk having gored.

"How far is it to the Pecos River?" a cowboy asked one night as he collapsed on his blankets and pulled his boots off.

"About three hundred miles yet to go," Ed told him. "And we're going to push these cattle as hard as they can go every foot of the way. They can stand it if we keep 'em watered." So far, they'd been lucky enough to find a few thin, trickling streams.

"And if we can't, how long can they last in this heat?"

"Don't even think about it," Ed told the man. "We have no choice but to keep pushing for the river. Between here and there, I can't tell you much about the likelihood of water. I never rode beyond this point, and I don't guess anyone else has either."

The cowboy who had shown concern was named Billy. He was a natural-born roper and horseman, and though he was the youngest man among them, he was respected and well liked. He could not have been more than sixteen, but when cowboys from different ranches came together to rope and ride in any kind of contest of skill, Billy often walked away with the prize money stuffed in the pockets of his worn jeans.

"Miss Starbuck," he said, "I got a feeling we'll find enough water between here and the Pecos River."

"I hope you're right," Jessie replied. She got up and prepared to get some sleep. Like her men, Jessie slept on the hard ground in her soogans, though she could easily have chosen to bed down in one of the huge supply wagons they had brought to carry water and feed.

Ki finished his meal and drifted away into the night. While he liked every one of the cowboys and enjoyed their conversation, he preferred to sleep and keep his own sentry about a mile from the camp. The hands understood, and even jokingly said that Ki guarded the cowboys who guarded the herd. This was, however, largely true; and the samurai thought it important that he distance himself at night so that his night vision was not impaired by the campfire. If there were Indians in this country, they would have excellent night vision, and the samurai had too much respect for them to put himself at any disadvantage. Besides, his senses were always sharper when he was alone without distractions so that he could hear and feel anything and everything that moved on across the ground. Not even Ki could do that when bedded right down next to five thousand restless cattle.

Ki peered up at the winking galaxies. He remembered when he was a starving child in Japan. His mother had been born to an aristocratic Japanese family. Ki had no pictures of her except those he kept locked in his mind. Even so, he clearly remembered her exquisite beauty, her long, shining black hair, and her heart-shaped face, which possessed the immense dignity and intelligence that resulted from untold centuries of royal Nipponese blood.

But intelligence does not rule the heart of a human being, and Ki's lovely mother had committed the tragic and unforgivable act of falling in love with a visiting American seaman, tall and dashing, who promised her that he would take her to his homeland and treasure her for the rest of her days. This had caused his mother's family great anguish, for the Yankee barbarians were considered a vastly inferior race. Though disgraced and abandoned by her own people, Ki's mother had not cared, because she so loved the tall American. Ki was born that first year of the marriage. Like most Eurasians, he was a beautiful child, the product and mix of the best of both races. But for five long years, Ki had known how it felt to be mocked as an outcast. Because of his mixed blood, he was shunned and despised by the other pure Japanese children of his own age. He had been an outcast, but nothing had seemed unbearable while his mother had waited for his father to return to Japan and take them away to the Americas. After all, his father had promised that, in America, all men were treated according to their abilities and accomplishments. Any free man could rise above the most dismal ancestry and become successful if he but had the heart, the courage and the unwavering determination to do so. Even as a small child, Ki had told himself that over and over.

But then tragedy had struck. His father had died of a blood disease just one month before they were to sail for America. With him gone, there had been no one willing or able to protect the Eurasian child and his disgraced mother, who was quickly cheated out of all her husband's assets. She had tried to seek help, but her own family could not find it in their hearts to forgive, and her husband's American family wanted no part of their son's Japanese wife, and a grandson whose eyes were slanted.

Abandoned by two countries and races, his mother had soon died of a broken heart, and Ki was turned away from every source of comfort because of his "impure blood." Oh, how he remembered the terror and the hunger, the accusing Japanese faces, the hurled rocks that cut his flesh, and the hurled taunts that shredded his spirit.

He had wanted to die, and might have starved to death had it not been for the old *ronin,* Hirata. Hirata had seen something in the starving child; maybe something of himself, for, though he was pure and noble of blood and birth, he too was an outcast, a samurai without a master, a "wave man," which meant one blown aimlessly, like the dying leaves of a tree. Owning nothing. Being nothing. Having absolutely nothing to live for but a samurai's code of honor . . . That was *ronin.*

Hirata had first tested him, though, tried to drive the ragged street urchin away. But, failing that, he had taken

17

Ki in and treated him hard, but with fairness. Taught him the ways of a samurai—not just how to fight, but how to live . . . and how to die—either in battle or with the sacred act of *seppuku,* or "ritual disembowelment."

*Yes,* Ki thought, *I remember Hirata and his lessons well*. Hirata had committed *seppuku,* but not until he was sure that Ki had learned the true samurai ways.

Overhead, the stars glittered like a field of scattered diamonds. Ki studied them thoughtfully—until the moment when he heard a sound in the night that caused him to freeze on his blankets and listen with every fiber of his being.

Horses on the move. Many horses coming nearer from the south. Ki rolled over, grabbing his bow and quiver. He listened carefully, making very sure that the horses were not those of the Circle Star's remuda or cowboys. Satisfied, he gathered his weapons and hurried up a low hill in order to see better. The moon was high, and the land was flooded with its pale light. But Ki knew well that these hills were covered with thick brush, and rolled like swells on a high sea. An army of outlaws could be within one mile of their camp and still not be detected.

Ki seemed to glide; his movements were economical and fluid. When he came to the rise in the hill, he flattened and eased over the crest to stare ahead, toward a large body of men coming silently, ominously, up a long valley. Ki counted no less than fifty riders. There was enough moonlight to see that they were all heavily armed. Comancheros. He was sure of it. Their horses were shod; had they been Comanches riding unshod Indian ponies, he would still have not heard the sound of their approach over the bawling of the longhorns and the sounds of the cow-camp.

Ki advanced down the hill toward his enemies. He selected "Death Song" as his first arrow. While staying low to the ground, he still managed to cover an enormous amount of ground swiftly. When he intersected the path of the Comancheros, Ki flattened on the ground and waited.

He knew he would not have had time to reach the Starbuck camp before the Comancheros attacked. Besides, this was more the way of the samurai—to strike with unexpected suddenness and to drive terror into the hearts of those who came to do ill.

Ki parted the brush beside the trail and raised his head. As always, he was without a hat, and his long hair was parted down the middle and held in place with a braided leather band. Slowly, he stood up and waited. The Comancheros were still seventy yards ahead, and the samurai was like a shadow they could not yet detect. Ki could smell the men and the horses now. Small clouds of dust rose from their hooves, and Ki supposed that that was how these killers had discovered that a herd was nearby. In this scorched country, five thousand longhorn cattle raised a cloud of dust that could be seen for thirty miles. These men must have seen it the day before, and had waited until night to attack.

Ki remembered Hirata's words: A samurai should wait until the moment he was seen before killing his enemies. And though Ki was trained in *ninjutsu*, the "art of the invisible assassin," he felt honor-bound as a samurai to wait until he was seen.

But this leader still did not see him. He was a large man with two bandoliers of bullets slung crosswise over his massive shoulders. Holding the reins in one hand and a rifle in the other, the man seemed to be looking downward toward the trail, searching for tracks.

"Stop and go back, that you may live!" Ki ordered in a voice that cut through the night.

Now the leader's head snapped up. He jerked on his reins, and his cruel Spanish bit cut deep into his horse's mouth. The animal reared in pain and the leader cursed.

But he had enough presence of mind to hiss a warning to his men: "Don't fire your guns, you fools! It is only one man."

The Comancheros crowded forward and saw the samurai standing alone in the moonlight. They were fierce-looking—scarred and lean, with guns, rifles, and knifes very much in evidence. Ki knew very well that Comancheros were more feared than *banditos,* or even Comanches. They had no loyalties, no weaknesses. They were like packs of wild dogs who would turn even onto one of their own at the first scent of blood.

The leader slowly raised his free arm. "Who are you?" he asked.

"A man."

"I can see that, you fool! Are you *loco?* What kind of a man speaks English and stands alone in the night out here with a bow and arrow?"

"A samurai. Turn back or die."

The leader cursed again, but without anger. One of his men said, "Let's leave him until later and come back and skin him alive."

But the leader wasn't listening. He stared at Ki as if he were some kind of ghostly apparition rising up in the night. "Tell me, strange one, are you with the herd of cattle?"

"Yes."

"Then be quiet and perhaps you might yet live. I think you are a crazy man. It is bad luck to kill the crazy. Step aside!"

Ki drew "Death Song" back until it shivered expectantly on his drawn bowstring. The talk was over.

The leader glanced sideways to a tall, thin man whose face was obscured by shadow. Ki glanced at him and understood. These men did not wish to risk a warning gunshot. So when the thin man reached for his throwing knife, Ki drew back his bowstring and unleashed "Death Song."

The sound of it has most often been described as an eerie, tortured shriek. Now, it grew in intensity as it streaked toward the thin man's heart. Its journey was short, but even in a split second its sound was so terrifying that the horses of the Comancheros bolted sideways in fear. And when the ceramic arrowhead drove into flesh, it exploded, and the song ended with chilling suddenness.

Someone fired a gun, and the sound of the shot reached and warned the entire Starbuck camp, just as Ki had planned. Dropping to one knee, he fired once more at the Comancheros' leader, and the chewer arrow ate its deadly way completely through the man's throat. The Comancheros unleashed a deadly hail of gunfire, and the samurai hit the dirt and slithered forward through the brush. The dust was thick, and they were expecting him to run. But with horses still whirling and men shouting, it was easy to move among them. Ki jumped to his feet, grabbed a man, then hauled him out of his saddle and buried his *tanto* blade in the man's chest.

A bullet seared its way across the broad muscle of Ki's back, and he spun and reached into his tunic. A *shuriken* star-blade glinted and whirled. Another Comanchero screamed and died.

"Forget him until later!" one of them yelled. "Let's steal the herd."

The cursing Comancheros were in total confusion. Bullets were flying about wildly, and one of the outlaws toppled from the saddle from a wild shot intended for Ki. But the samurai was back down in the dust and the brush, and when the Comancheros quirted their horses and galloped headlong toward the Starbuck camp, Ki was on his feet and racing for a riderless horse.

The animal spun away in terror at the strange sight and smell of the samurai. It started to run, and Ki pulled the *surushin* from around his waist. The *surushin* was a six-

21

foot length of rope with leather-covered steel balls at each end. He whirled it three times overhead and then let it fly. The *surushin* swept over the top of the brush and caught the running animal around its hind legs and sent it crashing to the earth. Ki was at its side in a moment. He unwrapped the *surushin* and threw himself into the saddle. He turned the dazed but frightened horse, whipped it smartly with his bow, and sent it racing after the attacking Comancheros.

The moon was at its zenith, and it bathed the hot prairie with light the color of melted butter. Ki had to rein his horse over to the side of the trail because the dust was so thick he could hardly breathe, much less see the trail. When he topped the rise and looked down at the big Starbuck camp, Ki felt as if his heart had stopped. The Comancheros were too smart and experienced to attack a big cowboy camp. Instead of foolishly riding straight into the ready guns of Jessie and her men, they were going for the big herd of cattle. It was frighteningly clear what they intended to do. They were going to stampede the flighty longhorns off their bedground and drive them right over the top of the Circle Star camp!

Ki groaned. There was no way to stop what was about to happen. The Comancheros were too far ahead, and they still outnumbered the cowboys. For one of the few times in his adult life, Ki felt helpless to avert a disaster. He would attack from the rear of the Comancheros, but it was up to Jessie and her men to somehow survive the stampede.

Jessie and her cowboys had considerably less than one minute from the first shot until the five thousand Texas longhorns jumped up from their bedground and stampeded toward camp. Billy was already up and going on watch, and his horse was still unsaddled. At the first sound of trouble, he vaulted onto his cow-pony. He had raced horses bareback as a child, and he figured he could do it again, in a pinch. He wasn't even packing his sixgun because he'd arisen still half asleep and it was still tucked into his bed-roll. Billy forgot about everything except turning the stampede. He dimly saw other Circle Star nightriders and heard their shouts of warning as they desperately tried to run the herd's leaders. Billy grabbed a fistful of mane and let out a wild Texas yell as he drove his horse into the longhorns.

He was no fool, and neither was his cow-pony. Together, they found a wedge in between all those long, wicked horns, and Billy swept off his Stetson and began thrashing the faces of those wild cattle. The other mounted Circle Star cowboys were firing their guns and whipping the leaders with their lariats. They were doing anything and everything they knew how to turn the herd.

They were only partially successful—too many cattle and not enough men. And as Billy screamed and cursed and whipped his hat, the cattle poured past him and thundered on toward the wagons and the campfire. Billy whirled his horse around and started back into the cattle. There were tears in his eyes, and he could not understand what had gone so wrong. He was shouting, but the huge cauldron of dust that enveloped him seemed to have a stranglehold on his voice.

Suddenly, he felt a terrible pain in his side. He slumped forward onto his horse's mane and hung on for his life. He did not understand what could have happened. The only possible explanation was that he had been gored. But when another bullet ripped into his powerful young body, Billy knew that he had been shot. With a numbness creeping into his extremities, he fumbled for his gun and remembered too late that it was still in his bedroll. Billy dropped his reins and gripped his racing horse's mane with both hands. His strength was like a river bleeding quickly into the desert sand. He prayed and hung on while his trained cowpony kept working the cattle. And when the stampede went through the camp and streamed on across the dry land, Billy let go and the moon went black.

Jessie knew at once that there was no time to run for their horses. No time to do anything except sprint for the wagons and try to shoot down the leaders and turn the herd before they leveled the camp. She shouted to them to run for cover, and they did. Cowboys in their dirty gray long-johns raced, barefooted and gingerly, firing back over their shoulders as the herd swept in. Two men who slept like the dead and could not react fast enough were trampled under by a sea of crazed beef. Ed, Jessie, and her men threw themselves behind the big supply and feed wagons and opened fire. They ground their teeth against their natural desire to save Circle Star cattle, not kill them. But kill them they did. The leaders crashed down and then flipped end over end as those behind smashed into their bodies. Hundreds of cattle went down, but enough came on to strike the wagons.

Men shouted in fear and helpless fury. They threw themselves and tried to keep the wagons from being knocked over. Tons of beef came driving in under the wagons—enough to lift them completely off the ground and smash them down upon the cowboys. Jessie fired until her gun was empty. The earth itself seemed to roll, and the sound of guns, screaming cowboys, and dying cattle filled her ears.

It seemed like an eternity before the stampede passed through her camp. In fact, the nightmare of destruction was over in less than three minutes. The crack of gunfire replaced the rolling drum of hoofbeats. Jessie looked up to see the Comancheros come sweeping into her camp. The dust was so thick and there was so much carnage of broken wagons that it seemed impossible that anyone could have survived the stampede. Jessie jammed fresh cartridges into her sixgun. A rider swept in. He wore a sombrero and was

24

looking for someone to kill, or a fresh body to loot. Jessie shot him out of his saddle. She turned and saw another rider, half-visible in the shifting darkness and dust. Jessie stepped forward and raised her gun.

"Ki!" she yelled. "Is that you?"

The samurai flew off his horse and raced to her side. He was generally reserved in his feelings, but this time he grabbed her and hugged her with joy. "I thought you must surely be dead!"

Behind them, more of the Circle Star survivors began to crawl out from under the wreckage and open fire. Being on foot, they had the advantage of a steady aim, and they began to empty more saddles.

The Comancheros broke and raced away after the herd. Jessie yelled, "Never mind the herd. Let's take care of our own men! We can catch up with the herd later."

By dawn's first light, Jessie knew their losses were devastating. Nine loyal Circle Star cowboys were dead. Billy was near death and could not be moved. At least seventy cattle were either dead or so crippled up they needed to be destroyed, and the rest were no doubt in the hands of the Comancheros.

"How many Comancheros are still alive?" Jessie asked.

Ki took a body count and made a guess. "I'd say thirty."

Jessie nodded. "Then they still outnumber us better than two to one."

She looked down at Billy. "I'm going to leave a man here with you until we get back with my herd," she said. "It shouldn't be more than two, maybe three days."

Billy nodded weakly. "If I die, please write my mother and . . ."

Jessie knelt beside her young cowboy and fought back tears. "Both bullets passed clear through you, Billy. Ki and

25

I have cleaned your wounds, and all you need is just a little time for those holes to close up and heal."

"But I want to go on with the boys to Santa Fe," he said. "I don't want to be left behind."

"You won't be. That's my promise. You're way too good a hand to leave behind, Billy."

The young cowboy managed a thin smile. "Does that mean I'm due for a raise, Miss Starbuck?"

Jessie managed to smile. Cowboys were always most irreverent when they were down or their backs were pressed to the wall. "Once we get through with this, you all get a raise. When the chips were down, you and the other boys fought like champions. It won't be forgotten."

Jessie stood up. She looked at Ki and she could see a terrible anger on his face. He had killed many Comancheros, but not enough to prevent this. Jessie lifted her chin and studied the devastation. She would need new wagons, and the feed would have to be shoveled up and reloaded. Another blistering day was ahead. The Comancheros now had four hours of head start.

"Let's bury our dead and say a few words over them," she told her survivors. "And then let's ride and pay back a debt."

Ki nodded and began to collect his bloodied *shuriken* blades and arrows. He had one more "Death Song" in his quiver, and he had not begun yet to use his *te*—"empty-hand fighting"—skills. But thirst was quickly going to become as much their enemy as the Comancheros. Their water casks were broken, and the Pecos River was still a long way off.

As if reading his concerns, Jessie said, "The Comancheros will know where there is water for our cattle. They would not have rustled them to see them die of thirst."

Ki nodded. That made sense. But then, Jessica Starbuck

was a very sensible woman. "This time, we shall see that they rustle no more," the samurai promised.

"Yes," Jessie replied, as her eyes drifted west toward the churned earth path that would lead them to her stolen herd. "When we catch up with them, they will steal, murder and plunder no more. I swear that on the name of my father."

"And I on the name of Hirata," Ki vowed. "But there may be others waiting."

"I'll give them a chance to walk away from a fight," Jessie said. "More of a chance than any of this group gave us."

Ki found a shovel among the wreckage. He drove its pointed head into the earth to dig the first grave. The shovel barely pierced the soil, for it was as hard and dry as flint. They would not take the time or use their strength to bury Comancheros; on the frontier of Texas, sometimes even getting a man buried was a sacrifice.

# Chapter 3

It was straight-up noon before the burying was done. The men stood, sweat-soaked and angry, as Jessie read a few lines from the Bible and then added a few words of her own:

"These men we've buried this morning were our friends. They rode for the Circle Star brand and died trying to save the herd. Each one of them was a top hand—a cowboy. They made good wages, but it was their code that made them stay in this line of work. They should never have died this way and—" Jessie felt an ache in her throat so big that she could barely continue. But she had one more thing to say, and it was important. Raising her eyes upward, she said, "Lord, I know the Holy Bible says turn the other cheek, but it also says an eye for an eye and a tooth for a tooth. I guess we'll take the last interpretation over the first. To my way of thinking, if they murdered my men, they've probably murdered or destroyed the lives of a lot of other fine people. So I hope you understand that we'll give them no quarter."

Jessie took a deep breath, and now she spoke directly to the bitter men who stood before her. Seeing all those fresh graves of young, good men made her feel old and choked with hate. Hate was destructive, Jessie knew that; but sometimes it was too natural, too powerful to control. And within the next few days, she knew that it would pass. It would have to pass. When she led her men against the Comancheros, it had to be with a cool, clear mind, one devoid of passion. Only fools went into battle out of control, and Jessie had learned from her father that fools seldom lived long on the frontier. *I will strive to be more like the samurai*, she thought. *Of all the men that I know or have ever seen, he is most in control and, therefore, most deadly.*

"When we find the cattle, we're going to strike the Comancheros and strike hard, but in a way that will make sure we win with the fewest possible losses. I owe you all that much, and we owe our dead compadres a swift and just victory."

Jessie knelt down and smoothed the earth on the grave closest to her. The graves were smooth to the ground and without even a wooden cross. In a few days, the dust would cover the fresh earth and they would be unmarked, unnoticed, and thus always undisturbed. "Cattle rustling is a hanging offense. The Comancheros know it as well as we do. So they'll fight to the death—no quarter asked, or given. There is one thing. The Comancheros know the land west and south of here better than anyone but the Indians themselves. They'll have to trail our herd to grass and water, and they'll have to do it fast. Ed Wright and I agree that we would be wise to hold off an attack until they reach water and feed. It might be tonight, or certainly no later than tomorrow. So we hold back a little and save our horses."

Ed added, "Speaking of horses, we've just enough for those of us going after the herd. The Comancheros were smart enough to catch up our entire remuda. Miss Starbuck's palomino will be their finest prize, and she doesn't want anyone taking any wild shots that might endanger that animal. Any questions?"

One grim-faced cowboy spoke up. "Miss Starbuck, do you expect they'll be taking our herd to trade to the Comanche?"

"No," Jessie said. "The Comanche don't have the money to pay for more than a few head of cattle. But they'll likely want to buy some of our horses—especially Sun. My guess is that the Comancheros will be taking the herd to some hidden valley or stronghold."

"Then I guess that means we might be taking on a whole lot more of 'em than hit us last night," the cowboy said.

"That's right," Jessie replied. "We may just be running smack into a lot more than we can possibly handle. That's why it's important that Billy and Calvin stay here and watch over things. Maybe you can even salvage something out of all this."

Billy and Calvin nodded. Calvin said, "We can make us a wagon out of the pieces. The harness is still all right. If we can catch us up some horses, we could follow along and—"

"No," Jessie said quickly. "Billy shouldn't be moved for at least a week. But if we're not back by then, I want you both to see if you can walk to Circle Star. Get a message to the Texas Rangers about what happened, and telling them that we have followed the Comancheros. They may be too shorthanded to come chasing all the way out here, but it's worth a try."

The two men nodded. "If the Indians don't kill us, we'll be here when you and the boys come back. Sure don't cotton to the idea of a long walk, ma'am."

"I didn't think you would," Jessie said. "But you'll have the chance to get in a little carpentry." Calvin was a good man with a hammer and nails. He also had some background as a wheelwright. He was the only man on the payroll who stood a chance of piecing together a wagon out of this kindling.

Jessie looked to her survivors. "Let's mount up and ride. We leave Calvin and Billy enough food and water for ten days. Two good rifles and enough ammunition to stand off a siege if any Comanche come by. We take everything else."

Ed nodded and got the men moving. Within ten minutes, they were on their horses and ready to ride.

Jessie rode past Billy and Calvin. "Good luck. We'll be back in a couple of days."

"We'd sure have liked to have come too," Billy said. "Don't seem fittin' that we should miss out on all the excitement."

Jessie grinned. "I thought maybe you'd had plenty enough excitement already."

"No, ma'am! Last night them . . . them fellas got in their share of licks. Now it's Circle Star's turn."

"That's right," Jessie said as she rode past.

Behind her, the samurai also said goodbye, and then each of the riders passed and called out. Some of their farewell words were insulting, and that meant that they were most dear. But some cowboys, still too shocked by losing so many of their companions, simply nodded and said a simple but heartfelt farewell. They all knew that these were Indian lands. A white man afoot or injured was in real trouble if he were caught by a war party. And the last thing any cowboy wanted was to get caught afoot. Every cowboy Jessie had ever known had felt smaller on foot than galloping across the plains on horseback.

All afternoon, the sun was like molten fire pouring down on them. It was the hottest day Jessie could ever remember, and it punished both men and animals. They had canteens, but that would not help the horses much. *No,* Jessie thought as the sun finally began to drive itself into the western hills, *we need to find water in a hurry, and so does my herd*.

Just before darkness the trail turned sharply to the north and angled around a series of low hills. After that, it began to climb a little, and when the sun went down the temperature finally dropped into the low nineties. The horses were tired and in need of water, so they stopped and emptied part of their precious water into their hats and let their horses gulp. It was pathetic how the poor beasts sucked up the water in just one or two swallows and then licked the wet felt material with their big tongues. Some of the cowboys didn't even want to allow themselves a single swallow, but Jessie made them take a couple anyway; a man half-crazed by thirst was not going to be any good in a raging gunbattle.

Ki knelt beside the trail and studied it carefully. "I'd say they're still about three hours ahead of us, Jessie. They're driving those longhorns hard."

Jessie had been thinking along those very same lines herself. "I know. If they were anything but Circle Star beef, we'd already be finding them dead along this trail. But as tough as they are, they can't go too much longer in this heat. It's been over twenty-four hours since we watered them good."

Jessie looked at her foreman. "I thought they might be heading for the Pecos River, the same as we were. But now that we've turned north, that doesn't appear to be the case at all. Let's mount up and move on."

At midnight they found water, only what was left of it was just mud. The Comancheros had probably raced on ahead and filled their canteens and let the horses drink first and then gotten out of the way. When a thirsty herd of longhorns smelled water, there was nothing in the world that could stop them.

Ki and several of the cowboys dismounted and began to

scoop at the mud with their hands. They worked and dug until their fingernails bled, and slowly shallow pockets of water emerged. It was slow, difficult work but every mouthful of muddy water was a lifesaving gift, and no one complained. Jessie took her turn with the men, and by daybreak the holes they had dug were three and four feet deep and filled with seepage.

To fill their canteens, they had to soak their bandannas and then wring them out. It took hours, but none of them were sure exactly how far the next water would be. If anything, the country around them seemed to be drier and hotter. They were riding up into the Texas Panhandle country, and the farther north they rode the less their chances of getting any help. This was Comanche country, and it might be such for a long time to come. Even the Texas Rangers conceded that there was just too damned much territory to make safe for families. Someday it might be settled, but that was still a long while off.

"If we ride far enough," Ki said, "won't we come to the Canadian River?"

"Yes," Jessie replied, "but we'll overtake this gang long before then."

"Not if they don't start finding better water holes," Ki said.

Jessie glanced sideways at the samurai, but she could not detect a grin in the early evening moonlight. Ki had an odd . . . well, perhaps different sense of humor from that of most men. It was, to say the least, very dry. And surprisingly, it surfaced most often when things were not going well. "I remember my father chased cattle up into this country," Jessie remarked.

Somewhere off to the west, a lone coyote howled at the moon. Ki waited respectfully until its song ended, then he said to Jessie, "Tell me about it."

"All right. It happened over ten years ago. A huge raiding party of Comanche struck our part of the country. They killed every settler they could and took white children slaves. They also took cattle, horses, guns, and anything else they could carry away on horseback. They burned and looted and . . . and worse."

"Was Circle Star hit?"

"Not directly," Jessie said. "They knew Father kept too large a crew. So they struck at branding time and killed about fifteen of our cowboys. Then they looted the chuck-wagon and took everything before they fired the wagon. It was three days before my father even knew that they had taken his cattle and scalped his men. I remember watching his face when he was told the news. Ki, you remember how tanned and fit he always looked. Well, right at that moment, his skin looked to be the color of ashes."

"I remember," Ki said.

"My father simply grabbed a rifle and went to saddle his horse. He had gone a mile or more before Ed Wright set the chase in order and formed up the men to come after him."

"It wasn't like your father to do anything ill-preparedly," Ki said.

"No," Jessie answered, "it wasn't. And before dark, he was back under control again. He led the Circle Star men for thirteen brutal days until he caught up with the Co-manche. He laid a trap for them and wiped them out just like they'd wiped out our cowboys. It was a hard fight; and when it was over, he spared one young Comanche warrior and sent him to warn his people never again to attack Circle Star. He told the boy that, if it happened again, he would come into their tipis and kill their women and children."

"I don't believe your father could have done that, given his conscience."

Jessie agreed. "Of course not, but it sure made an impression on that Comanche boy! It must have, because we've never been raided again. That's not to say it couldn't happen, but ranches all around ours have been hit off and on."

They rode for several hours in silence. Jessie was thinking about her father. How he had begun his empire so modestly with a tiny shop in San Francisco where he'd dealt in second-hand merchandise and a few items imported from the Far East. As his import business had begun to flourish, Alex had bought an old sailing ship to carry goods from Japan to China to the United States. He'd soon added a second and larger ship to the first, and then he had the beginnings of a small shipping fleet. From there, he had progressed steadily in the world of business and finance until his two ships became ten and he was the largest freighter plying the seas between the Orient and the United States.

Always a visionary, Alex had begun to think in terms of iron-hulled ships. He'd been one of the very first to convert his small but highly profitable shipyard into the making of iron-hulled steamers. Seeing the almost immediate acceptance of his then revolutionary shipbuilding techniques, Alex had expanded into steel-making, and bought his own mill. One thing led to another, and then he was building railroads to haul ore to his mill where he had begun to make steel rails for the first transcontinental railroad. For a decade, Alex Starbuck had concentrated on the burgeoning railroad system in America. He had purchased stock and even a controlling interest in half a dozen lines, and they were all enormously profitable. To finance them, he had also purchased a brokerage house and then several banks.

Less than twenty years after that small import house in San Francisco, Alex Starbuck had become one of the world's richest and most powerful men. He controlled and operated industries world-wide, and when he had been assassinated by a vicious cartel intent on overthrowing the American government, Jessie had inherited everything. She had never known her mother, who had died in childbirth, but Alex filled that void until his death.

There were some people who believed that Jessie was all looks and luck. That wasn't the least bit true. But sometimes she did yearn for marriage, children and many of the other things that women she knew possessed, and which gave them so much joy and satisfaction. But there were plenty of other times when she felt more alive on a worldwide tour of the Starbuck empire than she might ever be at home in the role of a homemaker or mother. And now, with this attack on the Starbuck cattle herd and the death of nine of her best men, she would not have traded places with anyone. Jessie wanted blood, and she was not ashamed to admit that the need for vengeance was sweet and strong. If that made her less of a woman, then so be it. Alex had not been ruthless but he had despised weakness, and there was something of that same attitude in Jessie. And on the Texas frontier, there was no room for weakness or indecision. There was right and there was wrong and there was damn little space in between.

Daylight came slowly over the land; at first there was just a faint light gray that touched the eastern horizon. But gradually the sage-covered hills became more than dark silhouettes, and as the sun rose, the sky flamed with crimson and gold. This was the finest time of day for Jessie. She loved a Texas dawn.

Jessie and Ki had ridden on ahead because the land was beginning to flatten out, and a single pair of horsemen would not be so easily seen by the Comancheros. They probably had no suspicion they were being followed. Not even the United States Cavalry would come this far north without a very desperate reason, and there were not enough

Texas Rangers in the state to face the dangers that would be found here.

"There's our herd," Ki said late that afternoon.

"Where?"

Ki pointed. "It's hard to see, but if you follow my finger you'll detect a cloud of dust off toward those brown mountains."

"Yes," Jessie said, "Now I see it! It must be fifteen miles away."

"At least." The samurai shielded his eyes for a moment. "The country up ahead is also gripped in drought. I cannot imagine where they are taking your cattle."

"Shall we wait for my men to catch up?"

Ki shook his head. "Let's try and overtake the Comancheros before darkness so that we can get a good picture of their night-camp. Maybe then we can figure out a way to attack and overwhelm them."

"If necessary, we can stampede the cattle again; only this time, it will be through their camp."

Ki nodded because he had been thinking of the very same thing. What was certain was that the Comancheros were far too large a force to join in an open battle.

By late afternoon, they found themselves climbing a low stairway of hills into the rugged brown mountains that dominated this part of the country. The vegetation changed almost imperceptibly as they rose above the flat Texas plains; brush grew a little taller as if it might receive more moisture that way, and the mountainsides became dotted with piñon and juniper pine. The trail was freshening, and by now was no more than two hours old.

Ki reined his horse in. "I think we'd better dismount and go ahead on foot. I can feel them up ahead somewhere in these mountains."

Jessie did not relish the thought of trying to keep up

with Ki on foot. Still, she had learned through hard experience that the samurai had a sixth sense about danger. He seemed to be able to feel its presence before it could actually be seen or heard.

When she dismounted, the rocks were hot and she felt them through the soles of her boots. She thought about her five thousand longhorn cattle, and knew that they were being tortured by this climb and the sun. There just *had* to be grass and water up ahead. These hills were so dry and forbidding in appearance.

Ki tied his horse and took up his bow and quiver. Jessie reluctantly tied her horse to another piñon pine and pulled her Winchester out of its scabbard. She followed the samurai up the twisting trail. The mountains were closing in on them, and there was something ominous about this country that raised the hair on the back of her neck. The trail itself was churned up badly by her cattle and the Comancheros' horses. But even if it had been untouched for a long time, there was something about it that warned Jessie that she was going into an evil, forbidding place.

There was no sound except for the occasional footfall that she made trying to follow the samurai. There was a breeze that offered some comfort from the heat, and yet it seemed to come at them from all directions, and it carried a strange, frightening sound. Jessie shook her head as if to drive away a bad thought. And yet the sound persisted from the labyrinth of canyons and steep rocky gorges that were filing off on both sides of them as they moved higher.

Ki heard it too. He stopped and raised his hand and held it behind his ear. He remained motionless for a long, long time.

"What is it?" Jessie asked in a hushed, expectant voice.

"I can't be sure but I think . . ." The samurai looked at her closely. "It sounds like a man crying out for mercy. It sounds like he is being tortured. I have not heard that sound since my boyhood in Japan when the emperor crushed a small rebellion and the guilty were hung upside down on crosses and their brains were fried in their skulls."

Despite the heat, Jessie shivered. "Let's go on," she said grimly.

The samurai nodded, but now he left the main trail and began to climb up the mountainside along a small game trail. It was difficult going and Jessie had to struggle. Sweat filmed her body and her breath came in bursts. She ground her teeth together and pushed on, knowing that Ki was going much slower for her sake than he would have otherwise. The samurai could match an Apache warrior for endurance, and they were the fittest men in America.

Hours passed and Jessie was nearly staggering with weariness. Her throat was parched when she finally stopped and said, "Ki, must we . . ."

The samurai froze and listened for a minute before he said, "We are almost there. Just a little farther."

Jessie struggled on, and soon they emerged on a high, rocky ridge. There was a spectacular view of the great Texas Panhandle country out behind them. Jessie could see for a hundred miles. She saw at least a dozen dust-devils, and guessed that one of them was probably caused by her cowboys. The wind was strong up here, and it felt good as she turned her sweaty face directly into it. Then she caught her breath, for there was a crying sound being carried by the wind.

"Ki!" she exclaimed, "what is that terrible sound?"

The samurai looked at her closely. "It is the sound of a man dying slowly," he said. "A man being tortured."

He moved swiftly toward the sound. Jessie picked up her rifle and hurried after him. So great was her trust in his senses that she had no fear whatsoever of walking into any immediate danger. But the screams filled her with dread.

Fifty yards up ahead, the samurai stopped very suddenly. He flattened on the rock and pulled himself forward. Jessie did the same. When her field of vision swept across the vast canyon below, it nearly took her breath away. They had found the legendary Comanchero Canyon that had been spoken of for decades but was never really believed in. This *had* to be the place where the Comancheros and renegade Indians came to hide after their bloody raids. Where they vanished as if they had dropped off the face of the earth, only to emerge again and leave a swath of death in their path as they burned and pillaged from Kansas to deep into Mexico. The canyon itself was truly magnificent. Not only was it impossible to see and therefore to storm by enemies, but it was an oasis. An underground water source bubbled out of the head of the great canyon, and the Comancheros had used slaves to make dams and irrigate huge sections of grass. There were trees enough for lumber, and Jessie counted at least a dozen shacks along with no fewer than fifty tipis. It was a cattle rustler's paradise, with corrals and plenty of feed and water.

"It must be at least ten miles long and five wide!" she whispered with growing excitement. "And I see Sun! He's grazing with our herd. And—"

The terrible scream that had led them to this canyon filled her ears and drew her attention from her horse and cattle. Off to her left, Jessie saw the man being tortured, and wished she hadn't looked.

The poor man was naked and very obviously the center of a crowd's rapt attention. It was a big crowd, too. No fewer than a hundred heavily armed men, some of them Comanche. Interspersed among them, Jessie saw at least thirty women, most of them young and brown-skinned. This was where young girls and women were brought as slaves to be traded or kept until they were no longer desirable. Most of them were from Mexico, but Jessie saw a blonde or two—probably the wives or daughters of ranchers and settlers.

"There is almost no way out of there except through the entrance," Ki said.

Jessie saw that the samurai was correct. The canyon sides were much too steep for anything other than a mountain goat to climb. Jessie figured the entrance would be guarded constantly. And the other end seemed to lead into a box that held no possibility of escape. The area below was so immense it was really a valley, but because of the box formed by cliffs, it was equally undeniably a canyon.

Another scream lifted on the wind. Jessie saw that the man being tortured was hanging suspended from an affair that resembled a ten-foot-tall hitching rail. His arms were tied wide apart and he was elevated just beyond the reach of the ground. A tall man was slowly, methodically stripping the flesh off his bones with a bullwhip. Jessie could hear the sound of the long black whip as it popped like a small-caliber pistol.

"I wonder what crime the poor devil committed to deserve that kind of fate," she said.

"I don't know," Ki answered. "It will be interesting to see what the bearded giant with the knife is about to do next."

Jessie had not noticed the knife-wielder. But now, as the one with the whip stepped back, the giant with the knife advanced and the victim begin to twist and thrash with uncontrollable terror. The giant stopped before the writhing victim, then turned his back on him and began to talk to the assembly of renegades and cutthroats. Jessie could not catch his words, but the snatches of them that she did hear sounded angry and blustering.

Then, he suddenly leaped forward and grabbed a beautiful Mexican girl from among the spectators, held her by her long, black hair and dragged her forward to face the shrieking man, who began to shake his head in violent protestation. The giant stabbed the tortured man in the buttocks, and then he slung the girl to the earth and brutally kicked her in the side.

Suddenly, another man jumped forward and struck the giant a hard blow from behind that staggered him. The crowd parted and made a huge ring for the two combatants. It was no contest. The giant was much the larger and stronger of the pair, and it seemed obvious even to Jessie that he could have easily killed the man with his knife. Instead, he toyed with him like a child, and then, shoving his knife back into his belt, he grabbed the man by the throat and began to throttle him with his bare hands.

The sight made Jessie half ill. It was clear that the smaller man had tried to protect the girl from the giant. Now he was going to be strangled to death for his gallantry. Jessie pulled her Winchester forward.

"No!" Ki said sharply. "If you try to save the man, we will be hunted down and killed, and so will the rest of your cowboys. There is nothing we can do to interfere in this. What goes on down there cannot affect us."

"I've never felt so helpless," Jessie said miserably.

"Watch the señorita!"

Jessie forced herself to look back down into the canyon. She saw the Mexican girl drag herself to her feet and then throw herself at the giant. In a rage, the giant swatted her aside. He choked the man in his grasp until the fellow went limp. Satisfied, he picked the man up and had him hung aloft like the first one—arms outstretched, feet almost touching the ground. When he was in place, he had the Mexican girl lifted up and hung by ropes too.

"This is getting worse every second," Jessie groaned as the man with the bullwhip stepped forward. "Now all three of them will be whipped to death."

"No," Ki said. "But I don't think the giant will kill them all. Maybe just the first one."

"What makes you so optimistic?"

"The señorita is too beautiful," the samurai said. "She is worth too much to damage."

Ki was right, as usual. The bullwhip was laid across her buttocks a dozen times, but she was wearing a heavy dress and Jessie could see that the force of the blows was minimal. It was being done for show and little else. But the second man was not as fortunate. His shirt was peeled away and he was lashed over and over. Jessie saw how his body twitched with every blow, and she could see the crimson blood fly. Most remarkable of all, the gallant man did not utter a cry.

"That one," Ki said, "is a man."

"But look," Jessie said with panic rising in her throat. "The giant has his knife out again and he's . . ."

She covered her eyes as the giant drove his knife between the first man's legs and publicly, inhumanly, castrated him. A scream ripped the canyon from end to end and then died at its highest pitch.

"The man is suffering no longer," Ki said quietly. "He has died."

# Chapter 4

The giant, Hector Oxman, was well pleased with himself as he hurled the bloody testicles to the dirt and ground them under his heel. He glared at the Comancheros and renegade Indians, and his mouth twisted into a cruel smile. "I will castrate any other man who looks twice at my woman!" he roared. "In fact, I will do it slowly, next time. Is that understood!"

The Comancheros were hard men, and the Indians among them were all killers and raiders. It took much to impress them, but now they were impressed. Each man felt his own testicles shrink upwards into the sanctuary of his groin. Gloria Morales was a beauty, all right, the kind of señorita a man would take many chances to possess; but no woman was worth ending up hung from a scaffold like a dressed beef while his gonads were sawed off.

The Comancheros' women were equally impressed, and most stared at the three who hung from the scaffolding. Several of them, still not deadened by the life of brutality they had been forced to live and to witness, were shocked by the sight of the castrated man. But the women who had been in this place for months thought it nothing special, for the Comanchero leader was known to be a jealous and mer-

44

ciless man. In fact, they all thought that Hector Oxman was an animal. But that was to be expected. In this hard land, only the strongest and most ruthless could survive. The Comancheros were like a pack of wild animals, and the only law in their canyon was the law of survival. For a woman, that meant you did what you were told without complaint—or you were beaten senseless. And if a man wanted to rut between your legs—any man, red, white or brown, at any time—then you lifted your skirts and satisfied him well enough that he would not beat you afterward. Men might fight and kill other men for your favors, but it would be *them* who died, not yourself.

Hector studied the crowd. He knew that he had their full respect and attention, but they were men who needed to be constantly reminded that he was their leader. "Gloria Morales is my woman, and the palomino is my new horse. As your leader, I have the right to take whatever I want, when I want. Obey me and you can stay and prosper. You are safe here under my command. But cross me, and you are finished. And you know this: Any man who tries to come or go without my permission will feel my wrath. *I* say who comes and goes!"

The Indians who understood English stiffened in anger. They were a free people, ruled by no man, not even Hector Oxman. They would come and go as they wished, and if the white giant tried to stop them they would fight him to the death. But even though they felt this, they said nothing, for they feared Oxman. He was believed to the strongest man in the world by the Indian tribes. Several years ago, Oxman had actually killed a bull buffalo with his bare hands. He had grabbed it by the horns and thrown it to the ground, where he had bent its great neck backward until it snapped like a dry twig. This was not just another white man's tale, but the truth, for it had been witnessed by several Comanche chiefs. He was also a deadly shot, and a great fighter who had demonstrated his bravery many times in battle. Hector was not a man who would die easily.

"Ross!"

The man with the long bullwhip stepped forward. "Yeah?"

Hector pointed to the castrated man. "Let his carcass hang for an entire week. I want it to ripen in the sun until the stench of it fills this canyon and reminds everyone that my word is law!"

"And what about the other two?"

Hector studied the young man who had attacked him from behind. Trevor Morgan was the fastest gunman among the Comancheros. He was handsome and bowed to no authority, and was therefore a real threat. But Trevor's father had led the Comancheros many years ago, and his fame was remembered. *If I kill the son,* Hector thought, *it could be thought that I was afraid of him. This I do not want.* There was another consideration. Gloria Morales might be falling in love with Trevor Morgan, and if he were executed, she was the kind of woman who could even try to exact a revenge sometime when he least expected it.

Hector Oxman feared no man, but a hate-filled señorita like Gloria could be dangerous. She could slip a knife into their bed and bury it in his gut or even his heart while he slept, or was on top of her and locked in pleasure. At such a moment, no man could be on his guard. Hector did not want to have Gloria Morales knife him, and he feared that he might have already put the idea of castration in her mind. *Probably,* he thought, *I should kill her and get myself a new woman.* But there was none to compare with her fire and beauty. She was the daughter of a Spanish nobleman who had backed the wrong dictator and been chased out of Mexico City to hide in a small village. She was educated and spoke perfect English. She could even read

46

and write, and Hector admired that very much. Yes, she was a rare prize.

He had been pillaging down in Mexico for years, and had taken dozens of young women, but not a single one had excited him nearly so much as the Morales girl. Not only was she the daughter of a Spanish nobleman but she was a fighter, a woman who vowed never to be broken in spirit. Hector had tried to break her many times. He had beaten and degraded her, but there remained deep inside her a strength that he could not steal. He was too jealous of the girl, and yet he did not wish for Trevor Morgan to remain in this camp to recover and challenge him to a gun-fight that he would not win.

Hector considered the thorny dilemma facing him. He could not spare Morgan without expecting a challenge, and if he killed Morgan and Gloria *was* in love with him, then she would try to end his life.

Suddenly he had an idea. "Cut Morgan down. Because of his father, I shall spare his life this time."

His first lieutenant was shocked by this display of char-ity. "But if Morgan had a knife, he would have buried it in your back when you struck Señorita Morales."

Hector lashed out powerfully and the back of his huge paw broke Ross's lips and loosened his teeth. Ross struck the earth and skidded to a halt. Hector stepped over to glare down at the man. "You do as I say without question!"

Ross wiped his bloody face and struggled to his feet. *Someday,* he thought, *I will kill this man—if Trevor Mor-gan does not do it first.* Shaken badly, his ears ringing, he touched his ruined lips, then signaled for several of the Comancheros to help him cut Morgan down and carry him to his late father's shack.

But when Morgan's body hit the dirt, Hector Oxman stepped forward. He grabbed the unconscious Morgan's gun hand, drew out his knife and sliced off the young gunfighter's trigger finger. Trevor Morgan groaned but did not regain consciousness. Hector tossed the finger away and grinned at the bloody stump with a good deal of satisfaction. The young man would not die, but he would never never again pose a threat with a sixgun, either. Hector chuckled at his own ingenuity. "Sometimes it pays to de-fang a snake, eh, Ross?"

The lieutenant tried to smile, but his lips were pulp and he winced instead.

Gloria Morales looked down and saw what the Coman-chero leader had done. She spat like a wet cat and tried to kick Hector, but she was powerless and he began to laugh at her helplessness.

"Damn you!" she cried. "You shall pay for that!"

Hector's satisfied grin died. He took his knife and pressed it to Trevor Morgan's throat. "If you do not be good to me, Señorita, I will slit him from ear to ear or castrate him like the other one. Which would you prefer?"

Gloria's dark eyes burned with hate and anger. She tried to spit at the man but her mouth was too dry.

Hector decided to cut the señorita down. When she tried to claw out his eyes, he swatted her alongside the head. Then he carried the dazed young woman to his place. He would inspect Gloria's buttocks very, very closely, and that might take all afternoon. He would remind her that he had spared her life and that she should be extremely grateful for his generosity.

As he strode away with the young señorita, men parted in his path. They did not miss the opportunity to look up her dress to the knees. Some of the men were so aroused by the sight of the helpless girl in the giant's arms that they grabbed Comanchero women and took them a little way away and then laid them down at once.

Hector Oxman did not come out again, and the warm afternoon passed without any further incident.

Jessie had watched the entire affair with a growing sense of helplessness. It was painfully obvious that there was far more at stake here than just her herd of longhorn cattle. There were slaves that needed to be saved from the Comancheros, and they would have to be her first priority. But the more she watched and the longer she thought about the situation, the more hopeless it seemed. There simply were not enough Circle Star cowboys left to successfully attack the Comancheros. Furthermore, by the time they could return to Austin and try to drum up support for a major army campaign, her herd would be rebranded and sold. Even worse was the likelihood that other slaves would be captured.

Ki looked at her. "I can read your thoughts," he said, "and for once, you seem at loss about what kind of action to take."

"Yes. Watching that brave girl down there made me realize how much of a responsibility we have to those women slaves. And if we attempt to stampede our herd through their camp, some of them would certainly be killed."

"This is true," the samurai said. "I think I had better try to get them out by myself."

Jessie shook her head. "That would be impossible."

"Almost," Ki admitted. "But it is the only thing I can think of to try."

"If you go down there, then so do I," Jessie said stubbornly.

Ki's voice was mildly reproving. "And if we are both caught? Who will ever know of this place? Who would save any of the slaves and stop the Comancheros?"

Jessie clenched her fists tightly. "You're right," she said. "We can't both go into that canyon. It's too risky."

"Then I shall go alone after dark. Maybe I can think of

something once I study the camp more closely."

Jessie didn't like the plan, but there was little else they could do. She glanced up at the sky. The wind had risen strongly through the afternoon, and clouds were scuttling across a darkening horizon. Maybe a storm was coming with rain. Ordinarily, that would be a joyous event, considering the drought they had endured. But right now, looking down into that green canyon, the only thing she could think about was that brave and beautiful Mexican girl and some of the other women she had seen being raped just a short while later, right out in plain view. It made her seethe with anger and humiliation.

"Can you get down from here?" she asked.

The samurai nodded. "I have seen a way already."

"I should have guessed," Jessie said. "All right. But if you get into trouble, I—"

Ki smiled. "You will need to ride for help."

Jessie touched his cheek. "You are always the logical one, Ki," she said quietly. "Answer me one question. If *I* were the one going down there and I were captured by the Comancheros, would you leave me and go for help?"

"I am a samurai," he told her after a long pause for reflection. "I could never do such a thing. My *karma* would never allow it."

"I see." Jessie said. "Then maybe you can understand why I could not leave you either. You're not the only one with an honorable karma. You're my dearest friend, Ki."

The samurai looked away quickly, for he was deeply moved and greatly honored. "I will do my best," he said. "But it would help me if you promised not to come down if I am captured. In fact, the thing that you should do is go back to the horses and wait for your men. Tell them to stay under cover, and that we may need to run for our lives tomorrow. Will you do that?"

Jessie studied his face. She knew that Ki did not fear

death if it was honorable. He did, however, fear for her life and safety. So now, if she refused to grant this request, the samurai would be burdened with unnecessary worry that might even decrease his already slim chances for success.

"All right," she said. "I'll go back to the horses. We'll be waiting at the canyon entrance in case you need help."

"Thank you," he said quietly. "I will try to save the girl. She will know how many others are strong enough and willing to risk escape."

Jessie thought that an excellent idea. She supposed there were many of the Comanchero women who would be too broken in spirit or health to try an escape that seemed all but impossible. Besides, even if they did succeed in leaving the canyon, what then? It was over a hundred miles to Circle Star or some army post which could offer them any hope of protection. And while she and her men could run and fight their way out of this country, they might not have any real chance to escape with the untested Comanchero women. Some would probably be poor riders and others too weak for the long, punishing race they would have to endure.

"Tell those who are too weak or afraid that we will return with help before a month passes and wipe out these Comancheros."

"I will do that," the samurai promised. "Goodbye."

Jessie and Ki waited until well after darkness to leave their place on the canyon rim. Heavy cloud cover still screened out the moonlight, and the samurai knew that once he reached the Comanchero camp this would be to his advantage. Ki moved swiftly along the top of the canyon wall until he came to a narrow vertical fissure in the rock. He eased down into it, feeling his way and knowing that one miscalculation would send him plunging to his death.

The wind had grown stronger, and the piñon and juniper

pines along the top of the canyon walls were whipping about. Ki hoped that Jessie would find the Circle Star cowboys waiting where they had left their horses. He grunted with effort as he began to descend into the canyon. The rock was not as hard as he had hoped. There were enough hand and footholds to work himself downward without great difficulty, but they often broke away, sending a shower of gravel down to the canyon floor. The samurai had removed his shoes, and he used his feet as well as his hands to lower himself downward. It was slow, difficult going, and midnight passed before he finally reached the canyon floor.

He untied the bundle around his waist. Unable to bring his bow and quiver because it would have caught in the rocks, he nonetheless had his *shuriken* blades and his *ninja* costume. He quickly changed into the black form-fitting suit, with its hood that covered his head except for a narrow eye-slit.

*Ninja.* A word that spelled fear in Japan. For centuries, *ninja* had been the ones called upon to use their skills as invisible assassins. They were trained from childhood how to utilize everything in the killing zone as cover, even the smallest of shadows. A *ninja* could sneak into castles and enemy camps and assassinate, then seem to vanish like smoke without any sign of his passing. Ki became *ninja* and moved like a cat despite the tremendous strain his legs were still feeling. The Comanchero camp was less than a mile away, and he knew that the camp dogs were now his real enemy.

Ki moved swiftly. He went from tree to tree, and when he reached the last of their number, he darted forward. A dog barked somewhere close by, and the martial-arts master dived headfirst into the tall grass. The dog growled and moved forward with the hair on its back raised. Ki pulled out a *shuriken* blade and held his breath expectantly. The dog growled again, but it was a hollow sound, without conviction, so Ki remained stationary for ten minutes until the animal turned and disappeared.

The samurai continued forward. He had seen the place where the bearded giant had taken the girl, and that was his destination. It would not be easy to get into the shack and awaken the girl without either of them making a sound, but if the giant stirred Ki was prepared to kill him in an instant.

A momentary break in the clouds confirmed his exact location, and the samurai slipped as quiet as a ghost into the middle of the Comanchero encampment. He had purposefully detoured the Indian camp, for he knew that they would have many dogs, and the Indians were usually more alert to danger than the whites or Mexicans. Ki passed the body of the castrated man, and he did not look up. He could almost feel the corpse hanging there as a grisly reminder of the savagery that existed among the Comancheros. What had the man done to deserve such a terrible fate? Ki suspected he had propositioned the señorita, and that torture and castration had been his punishment. And what of the second man, the one who had also been whipped, and whose finger had been cut off and thrown to the dogs? Was he too a lover of the señorita? It was possible and perhaps even quite likely. From what the samurai could tell, the señorita was desirable enough to attract many lovers.

As Ki tiptoed through the center of the camp, he saw men sleeping in the dirt, passed-out drunk. During the early evening, these men had gathered around a huge bonfire and had their rough fun among themselves and with the women. But now, the campfire was almost dead, just a few glowing coals that sent embers drifting upward whenever the wind gusted.

Ki saw the log cabin he wanted, and he covered the ground like a wraith. When he reached the cabin, he did not hesitate, but opened the door and stepped inside. It was very, very dark inside and it smelled of whiskey and cigars. He eased the door shut behind him and closed his eyes to better concentrate on the sound of breathing. When he heard snoring, he began to tiptoe forward, using his hands to feel for any unseen obstacles. He came to a wall and realized that this was a two-room cabin. Ki eased along the wall until he came to a door, which he gently pushed open.

Ki sensed rather than saw the giant and the girl stretched out on a grass-filled mattress thrown on the floor. He slowly moved forward in the darkness, and when he reached the edge of the mattress his hands moved up to the giant's skull. The man's breath was foul and he stank mightily. Ki remembered the savage callousness that he had displayed earlier, and he thought, *I should kill him right now.* Ki's fingers hovered over the giant's exposed throat. *I should do that and be finished forever with this one.*

But it was against his code of honor. He was *not* a true *ninja,* though he possessed their skills and secrets. Hirata, like other samurai, despised *ninja* and considered them dangerous to the extreme but unworthy of dignity. And without dignity or honor, a man had nothing. So instead of killing the giant, Ki's hand moved to the base of the man's neck and found the *atemi,* or pressure point. With great skill, he cut off the giant's flow of blood to the giant's brain, and induced him into a state of deep unconsciousness. The giant would not awaken until late morning. Ki had used this technique before, and it was so effective that the victim would not even realize why he had slept beyond his normal limits.

As the samurai's thumb pushed deeply into the Comanchero's throat, the man's snoring ended abruptly and his breathing slowed. Satisfied that he had done his work correctly, the samurai now moved around the mattress to the girl. With the giant unconscious, there was no longer much danger of her awakening with a cry of alarm that could spell a disaster.

Ki clamped his hand over the girl's mouth and placed his other hand over her throat. He felt her body jerk into wakefulness, and then she struggled.

"Do not be afraid of me!" Ki hissed. "I have come to help you."

The señorita did not believe him. She bit his hand, and the pain was great. Ki reluctantly found an *atemi* point and the señorita passed out, but the samurai knew that she would be unconscious only for a moment. He wondered if the reason why she had not responded to his words was that she spoke nothing but Spanish. It was possible. Ki frowned and reached into his *ninja* costume. He found a match and scratched it against his thumbnail. The match flared and bathed the room in a flickering yellow light. Ki saw a candle beside the mattress and he lit it. Then he studied the two figures. The giant was so immense that the Mexican girl looked like a doll beside him. She was naked, and Ki saw that she was well endowed and yet slim-waisted. Her legs were long and shapely, and in repose her expression was very different from the one she had worn when he had first seen her hanging from her wrists, which were now badly chafed and bloody. Ki gently rolled her over to see the angry welts on her backside. The bullwhip had not broken flesh, but it had come very close, and he knew that escape by horseback would cause her to suffer great pain.

Rocking back on his heels, Ki glanced around and spotted the señorita's ragged dress. He laid it over her, then began to pinch her cheeks hard enough to rouse her back into wakefulness.

When she stirred and groaned, he covered her mouth

once more and said, "I'm your friend. *Soy amigo, Señorita!*"

She relaxed. "Did you kill Hector Oxman?" she asked with only a slight accent to her voice.

Ki breathed a sigh of relief. "Then you *do* speak English. I was afraid I was going to have to murder Spanish."

"I *am* Spanish," she told him. "What are you?"

"Japanese and American," he said, surprised that the first words of their conversation should center upon their respective ancestries.

The woman looked down at her body and saw that he had covered her. "You must be the only gentleman in West Texas. Did you kill Hector?"

They both looked at the giant.

"No," Ki said. "I just put him to sleep. In the morning, he will not even realize anything happened."

She sat up quickly, not caring that the dress fell to her lap to reveal her breasts. "For Hector Oxman, there will be no morning. I will kill him myself."

She pulled a knife out from under the mattress. Ki grabbed her wrist. "Wait!" he said, tearing the weapon from her grasp. "I know you have every reason to kill him, but there are others who must be considered."

"Who?"

"The other Comanchero women. I want to take them out of here."

"You are plenty *loco* is what you are, Señor! You would not get ten feet before the dogs began to bark and the men awaken."

"I got here, didn't I?"

She looked closely at him. "What is that you are wearing?"

"It's a *ninja* costume." Ki had slipped off the hood, and now he slipped it back on for a moment to demonstrate. "It is used by assassins in Japan."

56

"Then prove it to me and kill Hector!"

"No," Ki said, removing the hood again. "And I will not give you the knife. Not until after we have talked."

The señorita stood up and climbed into her dress. She buttoned it up, her black eyes never leaving him. Despite the circumstances, Ki found her to possess such an animal magnetism that even he had trouble concentrating on the conversation until after she was completely dressed. But he did. Then he told her about himself and Jessie, and how they had followed the big herd of Circle Star cattle all the way into this forbidding country.

When he was finished, she said, "You and this . . . Miss Starbuck. You will never escape this land. They will find you and kill you slowly. It is too bad."

"And what about you and the other slaves? Have you all given up so easily? Can you say that there is no hope, no escape from this canyon, except in death?"

"I am too valuable to die, and so are many of the others," she said with a proud lift of her chin.

Ki shook his head. "There will come a day, maybe five years from now, maybe a few more, when you will not be as young or desirable. You must know that."

She lowered her eyes and the defiance in her melted. "Yes, I pray for that time, and my early death."

Ki was moved. This was not a display of feminine wiles, but a simple statement that life was so unbearable that death would be a blessing. "Listen to me. I have never done anything that failed. We have a chance. But we must move quickly and get others who might be strong and brave enough to escape. I can get you out of this canyon long before daylight. And if we can figure some way to steal horses—"

The girl shook her head, and her long, black hair waved back and forth. When she spoke, there was scorn in her voice. The scorn one would use to remprimand a well-

57

intentioned fool. "It is hopeless. They would catch us. Have you never seen the Comancheros or the Comanche ride?"

She was right, but she was also very wrong for giving up hope. Still, Ki knew that it would be impossible to get her and a few other women out of camp this night. They had already lost too much time.

Ki gave the woman back her knife as a gesture of his trust. "I want you to talk to the Comanchero women who are willing to try to escape. They can find a way to get us horses and we can meet tomorrow night after the men are sleeping. "We *have* to try, Señorita Morales! It is wrong not to at least try to save them."

Gloria drew a deep breath, and when she looked at the Comanchero leader, Ki was almost certain that she was going to cut his throat. He was just as certain that he would make no attempt to stop her again. But if she slaughtered Hector Oxman tonight, it would end all chances for any other of the Comanchero women to escape.

Gloria pitched the knife on the bed. "You are right, Señor. It is not up to me to decide who should have the chance to escape. I will talk to the women tomorrow. Where will I see you again?"

Ki thought about that for a moment. Jessie, of course, would be expecting him and the Comanchero women to attempt freedom this night. But when they did not, she would need to know that he was still alive and had decided to wait one more night. The only worry he had was that she might foolishly try to come into the camp in the hope of rescuing him. To avoid that disastrous possibility, Ki knew that he would have to slip past the guards at the entrance to the canyon and wait for her. Tomorrow night he would eliminate the guards before he returned to lead the women toward their freedom.

"Meet me where they keep the horses," he said, deciding out loud. "I will have chosen the swiftest and . . . Can you stand the pain of the saddle?" he asked, suddenly remembering the condition of her bottom.

Gloria smiled. "Ah! Then you saw the welts, and you are not quite the gentleman I thought, Señor Ki. But to answer your question—yes; if I can endure that giant Comanchero animal between my legs, I can endure a running horse, eh?"

Ki was glad it was dark because he felt his cheeks color. This señorita was not a woman who minced words or expressions. But then, if she were delicate of nature, she would already have been dead or crazed.

"Until tomorrow night, then," he said.

She reached out and touched him. "To make sure that you are real and that this is not all a dream, Señor."

"It's more like a nightmare for you, Señorita. But tell your friends that we *do* have a chance of escaping."

"How many men has this Miss Starbuck waiting outside? Sixty or seventy?"

Ki turned away. He did not have the heart to tell her that there were fewer than ten. "They are all brave and good fighters, Señorita."

She was not impressed. "So are the Comancheros and the Comanche. *Adios*."

"*Adios*," he said as he left her and moved to the bedroom door.

"Wait!"

Ki turned at her voice. She came to him and put her arms around his neck. Then she kissed his mouth. She was not clean; her scent was rank, and some of it was that of the Comanchero leader. But there was a raw desperation and hunger in her that made the samurai's toes curl, and he gripped her hard and felt himself deeply aroused.

Gloria Morales ended the embrace. "Now I am *sure* you are not a ghost or a dream."

Despite the grim circumstances and surroundings, the

samurai found it easy to chuckle. "I will be waiting for you. Trust in me."

"You and God," she whispered. "What else do I have to believe in?"

Ki had no answer. There was none in Comanchero Canyon.

# Chapter 5

Big, warm drops of water had begun to rain down from the sodden sky. Jessie carefully picked her way down the mountain toward where she and Ki had left their horses. She pulled her Stetson down tight as the wind ripped through the pines and the storm intensified. She knew she should be thankful for this rain, and she said a quick prayer that the storm would also be bringing precious water to her beloved Circle Star Ranch far to the southeast.

Thunder rolled, and jagged spears of lightning arced out of the black heavens. The rain became a deluge, and the rocks underfoot became slick. Each time that lightning crisscrossed the sky the entire landscape would light up, and Jessie would have a moment to see clearly. What she saw was not comforting. This was high desert country, and the arroyos and ravines she would have to cross would quickly become raging torrents of water. Well aware that she might even be cut off from their horses, Jessie began to hurry and take chances. She ignored the slippery footing, and in her haste she fell hard and often.

A bolt of lightning struck a tree just to the north of her, and the tree exploded. Jessie ran on. Suddenly, the trail took a sharp turn to her left. She missed it and crashed over the edge of a sharp precipice. She felt herself falling; then she crashed headlong into a torrent of water that was flooding down an arroyo. Gasping at the impact with the water, she swallowed a mouthful and choked. She was being spun around and around. The dark silhouette of a massive rock rushed at her, and she covered her face and struck it with tremendous force. The air was knocked out of her lungs, and she momentarily lost consciousness. The flash flood swept her downward, along with brush, small trees, and other living creatures which had not been able to reach high ground and safety.

Jessie choked and spit up dirty water. She blindly lashed out and caught a huge piece of wood and hugged it for dear life. Jessie felt her legs being slammed into unseen obstacles. Her lower body felt as if it were being ripped from her torso, and her legs quickly lost all sensation. She closed her eyes and prayed that the flash flood would soon lose its terrible momentum.

The big piece of scrub brush she clung to snagged on something and was ripped from her hands. Jessie felt herself rolling over and over, but then, all at once, the water seemed to slow. Very dimly, she realized that she had finally reached the broad, flat land at the base of the mountains. Her clothes were in tatters and she had lost one boot, along with her gun and its holster.

As the torrent of water flowed outward and lost its force, Jessie felt herself being rolled across sharp brush and stones. She tried to shield her face, but was only partially successful. Finally, she came to rest. That was when the real nightmare began.

*Rattlesnakes!* In horror, she felt and heard them wriggling in the muddy backwash all around her. They were slithering and shaking their rattles with deadly intent. Jessie recoiled in fear. She looked around to see them, but there was no lightning and the moon was covered by clouds. She tried to get up and run, but her legs responded like wooden stumps and she had no control over them. She staggered to her feet, tripped over something in the inky darkness, and fell again.

A pair of fangs bit into her forearm and she cried out, more in terror than in pain. Jessie threw her arms up and the reptile hung on for a moment. She came to her feet and began to run, and the snake dropped away. She charged blindly ahead, wanting only to get out of that snake-infested wash and up onto high ground. Another bolt of lightning lanced out of the storm, and she saw the higher ground she wanted. Mud clung to her boot and bare foot, and she tumbled into it face first. Then she clawed her way out of the arroyo. Panting and trying to swallow a rising tide of hysteria, Jessie ripped a strip from her shirt and concentrated on applying a tourniquet over the fang-marks. She reached into the pocket of her jeans and fumbled for the old pocketknife that had been given to her years ago by her father.

It required every bit of her considerable willpower for Jessie to calm herself. She reminded herself repeatedly that the chances of living through a snakebite were better if a person remained cool-headed and did not panic—and if they received help. Ed Wright and her men would take care of her if she could only reach the horses and find them in this sudden downpour. Now, more than ever, she *had* to find her men—and soon!

When the lightning flashed again, Jessie drew the sharp blade of her pocketknife across her arm. She already hurt in so many places that the two cross-hatch lacerations she made barely penetrated the fog of her existing pain. She pressed her lips over the bloody wound and sucked out what she hoped was most of the big rattlensake's venom. She could taste its bitterness along with her own blood. The taste make her stomach churn, and she suddenly

63

retched in the darkness. Beads of sweat coated her body and mixed with the rain. She felt a flash of cold run up her arm. Then it seemed to drive straight into her heart.

*I've got to get help!* she thought, pushing herself to her feet and stumbling forward. When she reached a small rise of land, she again waited for the lightning in a desperate attempt to regain her bearings. She remembered there had been a pointed rock, like a thin finger, very near where she and Ki had left their horses only yesterday. It seemed as if it had been a year since she had seen the samurai, and she wished with all her heart that he were with her now. He would know how to save her life.

She saw the finger! Jessie almost cried out with gratitude, even as she realized that she and Ki had probably hiked up the same wash that had swept her away only minutes ago. Therefore, it should not have surprised her that she was very close to the horses. With hope running strong inside her once more, she breathed deeply and ignored the steady throbbing that was beginning to swell her entire arm to twice its normal size while coloring it dark red. Jessie staggered forward. She tried not to think what she would do if Ed Wright and her men were not waiting just ahead.

With her breath coming in hard bursts and chills shaking her like an autumn leaf, she pushed on. When she reached the finger of rock, she grabbed it for support. When her head had cleared and she could move around the rock to the horses, lightning flashed. In that moment, she saw that the horses were gone!

Jessie groaned and stumbled forward. Maybe they had just run off during the storm and . . .

A powerful hand grabbed her by the throat. Lightning flashed again and Jessie looked up to see the flat, merciless face of a Comanche with his knife drawn back to scalp her.

64

Their eyes locked in that instant. Then darkness slammed down like a lid across the rim of the world.

The samurai felt the downpour on his face and watched the lightning play hide-and-seek across the vast Texas sky. Ki loved the rain. It rained much more in Japan than in Texas and he remembered as a child how green and lovely the carefully tilled hills were where he was raised as a boy. And the gardens and the flowers, so delicately beautiful that they seemed of another, softer world. He smiled upward into the warm summer rain and moved on down the canyon floor. There was little chance that a dog, much less a Comanchero, would see him in this downpour and raise the alarm. Even so, he moved with the darkness. When the lightning flashed and lit up the canyon, he froze and waited until it passed and then continued on.

He wanted to see the Comancheros' horses. They were kept nearer to the entrance to the canyon, although the Comanche insisted on tethering their best hunting and war ponies beside their tipis.

Ki had already determined that there was a pole fence across the entrance, and guards posted to prevent anything from coming or going without their knowledge. With the horses running free at this end of the canyon, Jessie's longhorn cattle at the other end, and the Comanchero and Indian camps roughly in the center, it was not going to be as difficult to save the Comanchero women as it had first appeared. Tonight he would find Jessie and her men and tell them of the plan. By dawn, he would be back inside Comanchero Canyon hiding again. Tomorrow night, if everything went as expected, Gloria would lead the women down to meet him near these horses. Then he would kill the guards and they would stampede all but the Comanche horses and run for safety. With luck, the women and horses would not even be missed until early the following morning, and by then they would have at least a four- to six-hour lead.

It *sounded* good. And now, as Ki moved close to the horse herd and surveyed the animals, he felt confident that they would be racing south into the Panhandle country by this time tomorrow. It was unfortunate about the longhorn cattle, and no doubt some of the Circle Star herd would be sold or eaten by the time they could return in force, but it was to Jessie's credit that she never gave a thought to the herd once the fate of the Comanchero women had become the primary issue.

A flash of light showed Ki the big horse herd. There were at least a hundred animals grazing nervously under the stormy skies, and they were skitterish. Even so, Ki hoped that the storm would last through tomorrow night and make it easier to escape.

He spotted Jessie's palomino, Sun, and slowly approached the animal. "It is me," he said easily. "Ki. Surely you remember me. Where is my pinto?"

The palomino did remember the samurai. It pranced forward, and when the lightning flashed, it seemed as if it were cast of pure gold. Ki patted the horse on its smooth-muscled shoulder. "I will soon have you and Jessie reunited," he promised. "Tomorrow night, you should be well rested and fed so that your strength and speed are once again second to none."

The horse tossed its head as if in answer. Ki saw his own horse nearby and went to the animal. He repeated his instructions, and the horse nuzzled him affectionately. The pinto was a superb animal, but it was no match for the palomino. That was the way it should be. If he and Jessie were running for their lives, the samurai would wish that

Jessie would pull ahead and leave him behind to fight and gain her more precious distance.

Ki slowly walked through the rest of the herd. He was extremely impressed with the caliber of horseflesh he saw all around him. There were no runts or crippled animals among the herd. They were all sound, most of them taller than the common Indian ponies, and they looked to be bred for speed and endurance. And why should that surprise him? The Comancheros relied on their horses to cover great distances in order to strike without warning. On the rare occasions when they were outnumbered and pursued, they always outdistanced their enemies. Therefore, next to their guns and gold, they prized good horseflesh even more than the flesh of women.

Satisfied that he could find fast, tough horses without any trouble at all, the samurai hurried on down the canyon toward its entrance. Now, aware that there were guards somewhere up ahead, he became *ninja* again. The hood came back over his head, and his black costume blended in perfectly with the night. He guessed that the hour was around three o'clock in the morning, and that because of the storm daylight would be delayed. That gave him plenty of time to exit the canyon, find Jessie, and then return to wait until Gloria Morales and the Comanchero women came to meet him tomorrow night.

Close under the rocky portal to the canyon a match flared, and Ki froze for a minute. The wind was moaning and tree branches were clashing like rapiers in the night, but he caught the snatches of desultory conversation. Curious to see the layout of their little rock guard station, Ki moved in on the men until he was within just a few yards of them. He crouched low and waited for a bolt of lightning to illuminate the entrance in its every silvery detail. Patience has its reward, and soon the lightning lit up the sky. The samurai blinked with surprise. The guards were not at ground level, but were hidden in a small cave about fifteen feet up from the ground!

Darkness blanketed the view again, but the samurai closed his eyes. The split-second image of the small cave used by the Comanchero guards remained vivid in his mind. How had they gotten up to their watchplace? Ki had not seen a ladder or any handholds chopped in the stone wall that a man could use to climb up the face of sheer rock.

The samurai was puzzled until another bolt of lightning showed him a rope ladder that dangled a few feet off the lip of the cave. So that was it! Ki frowned with grudging admiration, for it was a very intelligent safeguard against attack. The guards had a better vantage point from up on the rock wall, and they were almost impervious to attack.

*I will have to use my bow and arrows,* Ki thought. *It is the only way to reach them silently.* He was glad that he would soon have those prized weapons again. Leaving them with the horses had worried him somewhat.

Ki slipped through the pole fence. It was designed to be dismantled quickly for each new herd of cattle or stolen horses which arrived at the mouth of the canyon. Ki knew he would have no problem with the fence tomorrow night after he killed the guards.

Outside the canyon, he broke into a run that looked leisurely, but in fact covered the ground in short order. He knew exactly where to find Jessie, the Circle Star cowboys, and their horses. But he had covered no more than a mile when a warning sounded in his brain. He threw himself off the trail and into the brush. Just moments later, a small knot of Comanche warriors came up the trail. It was raining hard and their heads were bowed and they were covered with soggy blankets. They had ten riderless horses; two of them wore empty saddles and a third had a body draped over it, tied wrists to ankles under the horse's belly.

Ki let them pass on. Then he stepped out into the trail and began to run again. He had no quarrel with the Comanche, even the kind that frequented a Comanchero camp. All he wanted to do was to meet Jessie and then return before daylight.

Jessie was gone, and so were their horses. Ki swallowed a rising sense of alarm as he knelt and studied the ground where she had been captured. The rain had already washed away much of the storm, but there was enough that remained to fill his heart with dread. Enough to tell him that Jessie had been captured and their horses taken. Enough to realize that the five Comanche had been transporting Jessie's body across that horse, and that the two animals with the empty saddles were their own mounts.

Ki threw his head back and howled into the storm. It was too late to catch the Indians and save Jessie. Too late! She would already be in the canyon and reaching the Comancheros. And his bow . . . there!

He raced over to pick it up. Probably because of its unusual shape, it had been smashed across the rocks by the Indians. The quiver and arrows had been broken in pieces. Ki picked up the bow and saw that it was not seriously damaged, and that the precious, all-important gut string had not been severed. He strung the bow and tested its strength. It felt good in his arms, and hope rose from deep in his chest. Ki stuffed the broken arrows back into his quiver and whirled around toward the canyon. He could not overtake the Comanche and save Jessie before daylight, but tomorrow, while he waited for the Comanchero women, he could make new shafts and use the old feathers and arrowheads. He could still be ready tomorrow night, only now he would concentrate on saving Jessie before he saved the others.

That was the way it would be—unless the Comanche had killed her. In that case, Indian blood would flow from these mountains like fresh rainwater before he left Comanchero Canyon.

# Chapter 6

Gloria Morales had not slept at all since Ki's departure. She had not returned to Hector's bed; rather, she had sat on the porch of the two-room cabin and considered everything that Ki had told her. He was remarkable, she was prepared to say that much about him, for no ordinary man would have dared to enter this canyon. And to sneak right into the leader's cabin—now, that took courage and great skill. Even a Comanche might not have been able to get past the Comanchero dogs and invade the camp. But, remarkable or not, she doubted that any of this would come to a good end. Most likely, she and the other women who tried to escape would face the most severe punishment, perhaps even death.

Was it worth the gamble? Gloria did not know. Over and over she considered the alternative of not trying to escape compared to the consequences of failure. What was it the samurai had told her? He had said they had a chance to escape. And that, if she did not at least try, her beauty would begin to fade under the hard life of the Comancheros. And without beauty, Gloria knew that she was doomed. She would be unceremoniously thrown from Hector's cabin and another, younger, prettier girl would

71

take her place. A lieutenant would claim her and, after a few more years of hell and degradation, she would be thrown aside by him and made to grovel under a mere Comanchero. And finally, in ten years or so, she would either be dead or the squaw of some Comanche who would treat her far worse than a dog.

I have no choice, Gloria thought. The samurai was right. *I must* at least try. *And if we fail, then perhaps a quick death would be the best thing for me and some of the others.*

When dawn touched the eastern rim of the canyon and the rain began to slacken to a cold drizzle, Gloria Morales climbed stiffly to her feet. She touched her buttocks and wondered if she really could endure a long horseback ride to wherever the samurai hoped to go. *I will have to endure it,* she thought.

Gloria slipped back into the cabin. The filthy Comanchero leader would expect her to be asleep when he awoke. He liked to wake her up by crawling onto her while she was asleep and then taking her with brutal suddenness. He liked to see her awake, in pain, and filled with humiliation.

Gloria took the knife from the bed and stared at the huge man. *I must go with the samurai,* she told herself. *Or soon, I would slit his pig's throat, and then the others would make me die very slowly. And I haven't the strength to endure great torture. I found out that much yesterday with the whip, and the blows were less than hard. No,* she thought, shoving the knife under the mattress, *I must endure this man once more this morning and again tonight before I escape.*

She undressed and climbed into bed, and almost at once she began thinking about the samurai as the cabin lightened. Being educated, Gloria knew something about the world and the Japanese. Her father had once told her about the richness of the Orient and how the British had traded there for centuries. *It must be beautiful to spawn such beautiful men as that one,* she thought with a small smile on her lips.

Hector Oxman's snoring died. When the man stirred, Gloria closed her eyes, feeling her heart begin to race with fear. How could he possibly not have felt and remembered something when the samurai dug his thumb into his throat last night? He would remember and beat her into the admission that a man had come to their room. Of course he would think the man had come to make love to her. *Yes,* Gloria thought, *I will tell him that if the pain becomes too great. But then he will want to know which of his men would dare to do that after yesterday.*

*I will tell him that it was Ross, and then he will kill the only man in his camp who is truly loyal to him.*

*Yes,* she thought, *if he remembers what the samurai did last night, I will swear to him that it was Ross who dared to use his woman.*

She felt the giant roll over and climb up on his hands and knees. Felt his huge hand slide over the curve of her hips. A ball of ice formed in her throat, and Gloria forced her mind to go blank. To just detach itself from her violated body. But this morning, with the first ray of hope she had known since her capture, she could not blank her mind as well as usual.

She groaned. Her breath caught in her throat as he yanked her legs apart and drove his great rod deep into her. Her mouth flew open and he covered it with his own as he began to slam in and out of her dry and bruised womanhood. He reached under her hips and grabbed her welted buttocks and thrust even harder. The pain was so intense that she could not remain submissive. She bit his lip and he yelped and clouted her with the flat of his hand. She clawed at his face but he laughed at her and her struggles seemed to excite him.

73

Gloria looked up into his deep-set eyes and spit right into his face. It had the desired effect. With a roar of outrage, Hector Oxman doubled up his fist and hit her in the eye, and she felt nothing more.

The eye was almost swollen shut when she staggered outside later that morning. The rain clouds still covered the land like a dirty blanket, but here and there a break in the clouds revealed a small patch of blue. The wind had died down. Gloria moved stiffly down to the river, where she knelt and bathed her swollen face with cupped hands.

"I was afraid of that," a girl said to her. "He beat you again, didn't he?"

Gloria turned her head sideways to see a girl named Juanita. Juanita was her best friend, a pretty girl her own age from Sonora. "I had a secret visitor last night."

"Trevor Morgan?"

Gloria shook her head. "No, of course not."

"But he is in love with you and the only man brave enough—or maybe foolish enough—to die for your love. He looks at you like a sick puppy, and now that his finger has been cut off, he plots to murder Hector."

Gloria lifted her head with sudden interest. Such a man as Trevor Morgan, even with his trigger finger gone, could be invaluable in an escape attempt. But then maybe it would be foolish to risk telling him of the escape. The samurai had said nothing about trying to lead anyone but Comanchero slave women out of this canyon. And though Trevor Morgan might be in love with her, she really did not know if she could trust him with her life. What conversation they had conducted had been in hurried whispers. And even those had been reported by Hector's spies, and had resulted in his being whipped and cut yesterday. The poor man who had been castrated had been much less discreet. He really had dared to proposition her, and when she had told him to go away, he had grabbed her and tried to fondle her breasts. For this madness, he had paid with his testicles and his life.

Juanita looked closely at her friend. "Gloria, what kind of man would be so foolish as to visit you after what happened yesterday?"

"Will you swear on the grave of your mother that you will keep this a secret?"

Juanita nodded. She made the sign of the cross and whispered a few words, then said, "It is done. Tell me now."

Gloria told her everything about Ki and his plan. Juanita's eyes widened and she grew pale. "But that is so hard to believe!"

"I know. But I kissed him before he left and he held me close. He is a man, not a dream, Juanita. He will be here tonight to take us away if we have the courage to go."

"He will lead us to our deaths!"

Gloria shook her head. "We are dying *right now,*" she said harshly. "Look at me! Look at my face. Look in the water and see the reflection of your own face, Juanita. Like myself, you come from a small village. A peaceful village where all men are not animals and there are little children and maybe a priest and a church. Where are things worth living for. But here—" She threw out her arms and her voice was hard with bitterness. "Here there is only hell."

Juanita stared at her own reflection in the water. "You are right," she said finally. "I will come with you, and I will help you persuade the other women to come as well. Those who have the strength."

"There must be no betrayals."

"I know who can be trusted with our lives," Juanita said a little defensively.

Gloria took a deep breath and let it out slow. "This samurai. He may need a man's help with the horses and the

75

fighting. I have been thinking of asking Trevor Morgan to help. What do you think?"

Juanita looked back toward the camp. "He is brave, and is said to be a great fighter; even with only nine fingers that should still be true. I think you must dare to do that. He loves you. He would not betray you to a certain death."

Gloria patted her face dry with her hands. Even more important than Morgan's obvious love for her was the hatred he felt for Hector Oxman. He would rather have his tongue cut out than help that man.

"If you see him, tell him to meet me in those trees at noon, where we can talk alone for a few minutes."

Juanita shook her head. "There is too much risk! Let me tell him of this samurai."

"All right. You tell him. Say that our lives are at stake and that if he does not want to help us I pray that he will not hurt us either, and that he will let us go to whatever fate is ahead."

"I will do that," Juanita promised. "And tonight, where shall we meet this . . . What does he call himself?"

"A samurai," Gloria said, raising her chin. "He comes from a noble people far across the sea. He wears a black outfit, like a man would sleep in."

"And many guns, I hope?"

Gloria frowned. Thinking about it now, she had not seen any weapons on the samurai. "He will have many guns," she promised, knowing that Juanita needed that assurance. "And I think he might slit Hector's throat for me before we leave."

Juanita crossed herself again. "God would like that," she whispered. "Until tonight, then!"

But it was not to be. Late that afternoon, there was great excitement in camp when Pale Horse, leader of the renegade Comanche, brought a bunch of his best warriors into the Comanchero camp. Because Pale Horse was a chief and it was beneath his dignity to seek out the leader of the Comancheros directly, he sent his men to find Hector and bring him forward. When the two leaders stood face to face, Pale Horse bragged that he had captured a white woman and two saddled horses just outside the canyon. He seemed very pleased with himself, and it was plain that he thought that the Comancheros were growing unwary to allow such a thing to occur.

Hector's face displayed anger and disbelief. He glanced toward his men and they shrank back, none wanting to face their leader's anger. Besides, this did seem impossible, and most thought that Pale Horse was lying, a thing he was known to do. No white man or woman had ever come this deep into their Texas Panhandle stronghold without permission. If such a woman really existed, then she must be the slave of one of their members. Comancheros were always raiding somewhere, and this woman had to belong to one of them.

"I want to see her!" Hector demanded.

"She is very ill, maybe to death. Snakebite. Very bad. Medicine man say could die."

"She has to belong to one of my men!" Hector said.

"She belongs to me," the chief replied. "She will be *my* woman!"

The two killers stood across from each other. The Comancheros were lined up against the Indians who had come with their chief. This could spell disaster, and every man knew it. If Hector killed Pale Horse, which he most certainly would, then there would be open war between the Comanche and the Comancheros. This must not be.

Hector knew this as well. He had great power, but that power came largely from his alliance with the Comanche. To break that alliance would be to find himself and his men in constant peril. There were too many Comanche, and they would enlist the Kiowa as well. So Hector, despite his pride, had to find a way to back down.

"Is she young and desirable?" he asked, being a man of few subtleties.

"Ugly and too skinny."

This raised Hector's suspicions and made him more determined to see the new captive woman. "I like skinny squaws. Maybe I trade you for a nice, fat Mexican woman," Hector said with a wide grin.

Pale Horse did not seem greatly enthused by the idea. "My new woman have golden hair."

"Yes," Hector replied. "But she may die, and then you will have nothing but a pretty scalp-lock to hang on your lance. Show me the woman and I trade you if I like."

Pale Horse considered this demand carefully. He too did not want to fight because he was not equal to the Comanchero leader's renowned strength. Better to trade, perhaps, and live, than to die for a woman who might die of poisoning anyway. Besides, her face was ugly. Too much blood and scratches. "I bring her to you on travois tomorrow," he grunted.

"Today," Hector insisted. "I want to see her before any of your braves sneak into your tipi and use her."

Pale Horse was greatly insulted. He bristled, and his warriors stiffened in preparation to die—for die they most certainly would in this canyon where they were outnumbered and outgunned. "I bring after drink of firewater," Pale Horse said, salvaging his own pride. "You bring for me and my warriors. Pronto!"

Hector signaled Ross to bring a bottle. The Comanchero lieutenant returned a few minutes later and handed the bottle of whiskey to his leader. Hector bit the cork with his teeth and then spat it to the earth. He took a long pull, and then wiped his mouth with the back of his sleeve. "Just doin' it to prove I ain't poisoned the bottle, Pale Horse.

More than one redskin has been poisoned by someone acting like a friend. Now you know that the whiskey is good." He extended the bottle to the Comanche chief. "Now tell your men to bring the white woman for me to inspect."

Pale Horse studiously ignored the command. He drank well before he turned and signaled for the woman to be brought into the Comanchero camp.

The Comanchero women were immediately seized by the grip of terror. If the white woman was more desirable than any one of them, then they would be traded to the Comanche, and that would be the end. The Comancheros were bad, but the Comanche were far worse, and their squaws beat, pinched, and made life unbearable for white or Mexican slave women.

Gloria Morales was sick to her stomach, for she knew this was the samurai's woman. That meant there was less chance for escape. In fact, it was possible that the samurai had become disheartened by the loss of his woman and gone away. Gloria would have to give this some thought. But no matter what, this capture of the white woman was not good. She did not want any of the Comanchero women to be traded away to a fate worse than death.

Trevor Morgan was also deeply troubled. He had listened with great interest to Juanita's whispered story, and though it seemed impossible that this . . . this strange samurai from across the world had actually managed to slip into the Comanchero camp, he knew that Gloria Morales would not risk their lives for nothing. So he was prepared to leave with the Comanchero women, for he had seen enough death, torture, and degradation to last his lifetime. He wanted out. But that was not an easy thing to do, especially now that he had lost his trigger finger and was no longer feared or particularly respected. That would change in time, for he had already discovered that he could draw and fire his sixgun with his middle finger quite well. Unfortunately, "quite well" was not good enough to beat Oxman and some of the best of these bloody dogs. However, in time, Trevor was certain he could regain his form and speed with a sixgun. And when that moment came, he would kill Hector Oxman and try to take Gloria Morales home to her village in Old Mexico. Only now everything had changed with the discovery of those horses and the snakebit white woman.

It seemed like hours before the Indians returned with a travois and the woman covered from her chin to her toes with dirty blankets. Everyone crowded around her and stared. Seeing her scratched face and tangled, dirty hair, most of the Comanchero women felt a deep sigh of relief. Besides, from her color, she looked to be almost dead.

Hector Oxman reached under the blanket, pulled out the hugely swollen and black arm and lost all interest—the woman was going to die.

He grabbed her face and pinched her cheeks between his thumb and forefinger. "Who are you, and who brought you to my canyon?"

Jessie roused into wakefulness. She was drenched with sweat and shaking violently despite the blankets. She had to squint her eyes to bring the giant into focus. One look at him, however, brought all the memories of the three hanging from the scaffold, of the castration, whipping, and torture. It brought her to full wakefulness. Jessie steeled herself and looked up into his pitiless eyes. She had heard the question, but she feigned confusion to buy herself a few precious moments to think.

"Answer me, damn you!" Hector raged. "How did you get here? Who brought you here, and what happened to him?"

Jessie swallowed. He thought that she was a captured slave! "I don't know his name. He . . . he was drowned in

80

the flood. We were caught sleeping in an arroyo last night, and when I woke up, I got snakebit."

"Only a fool would sleep in an arroyo under cloudy skies!" Hector Oxman raged. "What's your name, woman?"

"Jessie."

He grabbed her again. "Jessie who, from where?"

She did not have the strength to so much as struggle against him. His fingers bit deeply into her cheeks and she wanted to fight back tears. She needed time to *think*, dammit! And she couldn't think with her head spinning and her body on fire from the poison. Jessie pretended to faint.

The giant cursed. "She's almost sure to die and I say it's no loss. Sure would have liked to have known which of my men it was that brought her here, though. You can keep her, Pale Horse. You'll bury her by morning."

Pale Horse secretly agreed. He was angered and ashamed, for when a woman slave was not seen as being worth anything by another man, it lost him face and value. He would be disgraced to keep this woman when Oxman had tossed her aside as being worthless. And even though his medicine man had said she would live, she had lost her appeal.

"I trade for her," Pale Horse said, pointing at Juanita, who recoiled in fear.

"Hell, no!" Oxman growled. He looked at his men. "Any of you want this dying woman for one night enough to trade something to Pale Horse?"

The Comancheros shook their heads and stared at the discolored arm. What good was a corpse when there were healthy women in camp?

"Pale Horse, I'll trade a gun for her," Trevor Morgan said, stepping forward. "It's old, but anyone here can tell you it shoots damn straight."

Hector Oxman blinked with surprise. Then he laughed

81

outright. "No finger, no guts, huh? What are you going to do without your gun, cook for my men?"

Morgan's cheeks flamed. "I got another gun that I'm going to show you some day soon," he said in a voice so ominous that no one could fail to understand his deadly intentions.

Oxman stiffened. "Why don't you run and get it right now?"

Morgan shook his head. "Not yet." He turned to the Comanche chief and unholstered his sixgun. He extended it, butt first. "It works fine," he said. "The gun for the dying woman."

Pale Horse could not believe this sudden turn of good fortune. A moment ago he had lost face and was saddled with a thing of no value. Now he had a fine Colt revolver. He tried not to grin, but only half succeeded. "Deal, Morgan. Woman yours!"

"Then I'll take her to my place right now. If you got a medicine man that's been giving her any potions, tell him to keep sending them along because I know you people have good medicine. Besides, if the woman dies anyway, at least I can use them to soak the stump of my trigger finger."

Oxman laughed at that little self-deprecating joke, and his men laughed too. Even the Comanche smiled and breathed a sigh that their leader had not been shamed.

It all seemed to work out well.

★

# Chapter 7

Jessie felt herself being lifted in Trevor Morgan's strong arms. She did not open her eyes as he carried her through the crowd of red and white men toward his cabin, the cabin that had been his father's before him. Jessie still could not believe that the giant Comanchero had allowed her to go without further harm or questions. She dimly realized that her good fortune rested entirely upon the man who now placed her down upon his bed.

She pretended to be in a faint, but he saw through that and went to the stove, where he picked up a steaming pot of coffee and said, "You might feel better with a cup of coffee, Jessie. The Comanche medicine man gave me some roots and herbs to boil and use as a poultice on that arm. Must have been a real grand-daddy of a rattlesnake to have put so much poison in you."

Jessie opened her eyes, knowing it was pointless to pretend she did not hear him. But she was very weak as she pushed herself up on one elbow and said, "I cut the wound and tried to suck out the venom, but I don't seem to have done much of a job."

He brought her a cup of coffee and said, "You got a small arm and he had long fangs. Sucking on the wound doesn't work very well when that's the case. But the Comanche medicine man musta thought you'd pull through all right."

"What makes you think so?"

Trevor Morgan helped her to sit up and drink. "A medicine man, no matter what tribe he belongs to, he don't much want to lose patients. Makes it look as if his power is weak. So a smart one like old Thunder Rolls out there, he musta figured you were salvageable or he wouldn't have bothered to doctor you."

Jessie said nothing. She looked around the interior of the Comanchero's cabin with both interest and apprehension. She had no idea why he had traded his gun for her, but if it were for his pleasure, he was damn sure going to wish he had his gun back, *muy pronto.*

The cabin was a surprise. It wasn't exactly clean, but neither was it the pigsty she'd expected. Besides the bed she was lying upon, there was a table and two chairs, a few pictures on the wall, and even a feed-sack curtain over a real glass window, and a shelf of books. The stove was a converted iron barrel. The cabin had a dirt floor, but it was swept. Things were neatly put in place, and he had an arsenal of firearms. At a glance, Jessie counted three or four pistols and at least as many rifles, all of them oiled and in good order.

"What do you think?" he asked, with a look of amusement. "'Bout what you'd expect a Comanchero's cabin to be like?"

"Not at all," she admitted, being surprised by the neatness and order of the room, and thinking he must have a woman but seeing no real evidence of the fact. "You're very different than those men outside."

He shrugged. "I've killed my share of men," he said with a frown. "Don't be misled."

"I'm not," Jessie told him, "but you're the man that

84

tried to save that girl from more of a whipping."

He turned away, and when he spoke, his voice was sharp and cutting. "Yeah, that was me all right. And look what I got for it—no finger, and a back that will take a month to heal."

He turned, and she noticed that he did move stiffly. Carrying her, stretching out his muscles as he had done, must have been extremely painful, and yet he had not said a word.

"Why did you trade for me?"

"Because the gun wasn't worth much," he said impassively.

"That's not the reason!"

"All right. I did it because I know who you really are. You're Jessica Starbuck and you own all those cattle that we're changing the brands on."

Jessie had not wanted her true identity known, for then the Comancheros would be sure to hold her for some outrageous ransom. But he seemed so sure of himself that she knew there was no sense in denying the truth. "So why didn't you tell your leader?"

"Maybe I want a ransom all for myself."

That made sense. "How much?"

"You're a very rich woman, aren't you?"

"Providing I live through whatever is going to happen in this canyon, how much?"

He smiled. "After hearing what a girl named Juanita told me last night, I'd say that your samurai faces damn long odds. In fact, I don't think you have any chance at all of getting yourselves out of this canyon alive, much less this part of Texas."

"So you know everything," Jessie said, trying to hide her disappointment.

"The Comanchero women have decided to trust me—I guess because I tried to save Gloria Morales yesterday. Or

85

maybe they're so desperate that they have no choice. Anyway, I want you to tell me exactly what you have in mind."

Jessie sipped at the coffee. It was strong enough to corrode horseshoe nails, but it set well on her stomach and gave her a lift. She looked directly into the Comanchero's brown eyes and said, "Before I decide to answer that question, were you on the raid that stole my herd and stampeded my crew to death?"

"No. I was here. I used to do things like that, though. Like I said, I've killed more than my share."

"But not anymore?"

His eyes narrowed a little, and his mouth formed a hard, thin line. "The next man I kill will be Hector Oxman."

"For his woman?"

Trevor Morgan laughed outright. "You saw it all, didn't you?"

"Yes, the samurai and I were up on the rim, watching. That's why I think I can trust you with the truth."

"You have no choice *but* to trust me, lady! You're in an even worse mess than Gloria and the others. If Hector learns who you really are—"

"Don't say it," Jessie told him. "I think I can guess. I saw what he did to the other man he put up to hang."

Trevor looked away quickly. "My father was known as a hard man, and a killer, too, but he wasn't vicious. He just took what he wanted and he let those without anything be. Oxman likes to hurt people and things. He likes the sight of blood and suffering. The bastard makes me sick."

"Then why don't you just leave?"

"No one leaves without permission."

Jessie did not believe the man. "If you wanted to escape, I don't doubt for a minute that you could."

He poured himself the dregs of his coffeepot and took a chair beside the table. He leaned back, cocked a leg over his knee, and studied her with interest. "I saw you in San

Antonio once, Miss Starbuck. About a year ago. I knew you were the most beautiful woman I ever saw in my life. I watched you and some tall gentleman in a fine suit ride by in a carriage, and I knew that I wasn't ever going to have myself a woman to compare. I'm not on your level, but then, neither is anyone else in this canyon, or most of Texas."

"What are you trying to say?"

He jammed his fists into his pockets and stared at her. "That I don't trust you not to just turn me over to the hangman, even if I help you and those women reach Circle Star."

Jessie shook her head back and forth. "Not only would I not turn you in, but I'd give you a job and the chance to go straight. A Comanchero has certain skills that are valuable on a cattle ranch."

"You mean like using a running iron?"

"Of course not! But you must be good with horses, guns, and cattle. I can always use good men, and I never forget loyalty."

He chuckled. "So that's the offer, huh? No ransom, just a job."

"A chance to start over is what I'm offering you!" Jessie snapped. "And if you've killed a lot of innocent people already, this would be your one opportunity to wipe the slate clean. To save lives and earn yourself some peace of mind. Because what you are and what you've done is eating you up inside, isn't it?"

"Yes, dammit! I'm sick and tired of the murdering and the torture. Everyone in this camp rides with a ball of fear in his belly. And the women . . . I remember my mother."

He glared at her. He was a handsome man with a cleft in his chin and wavy brown hair and intelligent eyes. But he was also very angry. "Yeah, Miss Jessica Starbuck," he said in a tight voice, "even a Comanchero once had a mother. Mine lived right in this cabin until about a year after my father was killed during a raid. After that, my mother seemed to wither and fade. She wanted to make things better for the slaves brought here. And she tried, but it was no good. Oxman ridiculed her, and his men made her feel small and old. I used to want to kill them all, but now the only one I want to get is Oxman himself."

"Then we ought to help each other," Jessie said in her most reasonable tone of voice. "Because the samurai is out there somewhere, and he's coming for me."

"What happened to your crew?"

"Many of them were killed during the stampede. My foreman and some of the survivors were hurt, and I wanted them to stay back while Ki and I traveled up ahead. I don't know what happened to them. I expected to find them last night, but they were gone."

"They must have gotten lost," Trevor said. "The wind blew out your tracks and the rain finished the job. They've probably been seen by Comanche by now and scalped."

Jessie had not thought of that possibility, but it was very real. White men simply did not ride around in this Indian country—not unless they were part of a large army. Ed Wright and her few remaining cowboys would search valiantly for days to find her, but failing that, the foreman would have enough sense to go back to get Billy and Calvin and then head for the ranch before he was spotted by a huge party of Comanche.

"You didn't want to hear that, did you? I'm real sorry, but this is sudden killin' country. There's nothing out there that lives without the Comanche knowing and approving of it. What's left of your crew is dead, I tell you. You might as well face up to it, and then we'll go from there."

Jessie looked up. "We?"

"Yeah," Trevor said. "You heard right. I'm going to

take you up on that job offer. But we'll have to wait about a week."

"Why?"

"Because you aren't fit to ride, and neither is Gloria Morales, though she won't admit the truth any more than you. No matter how hard you and Gloria tried, you'd slow everyone down. That would get us killed for certain. It'll take a good week, maybe longer, to work something else out, and if it isn't right the first time, there won't be any second chances."

"Ki has to know what happened."

"How you going to find him?" Trevor asked.

"He'll find us," she said. "Tonight."

The Comanchero looked at her skeptically. "If he gets back down here and inside this cabin before me or anyone else sees him, he is a pretty special piece of work, all right."

"Oh," Jessie said, "he's very special. He'll protect me with his life."

Trevor wasn't impressed. This so-called samurai had allowed his boss to get herself half drowned, bitten by a rattlesnake, and captured by the Comanche. That didn't seem very impressive at all. Maybe what this rich young woman needed was a *real* bodyguard and protector.

"You came within a hair of losing your life last night, Jessie. I guess even a man with nine fingers could do a better job than your samurai."

Jessie knew not to argue with the man. He was young and tormented, and he needed to believe in himself. When Ki showed up tonight, the very act of getting here unseen would speak volumes for his extraordinary ability.

"I do feel weak and sick," she told him. "I'm going to sleep for a while. Ki will wake me up when he arrives."

"Like hell he will," Trevor said bluntly. "*I'll* be the one who wakes you. If he somehow manages to get past the guards, the Comancheros, the Comanche, and all the camp dogs again."

"He will, Trevor," she said closing her eyes. "He most certainly will."

The samurai had spent an anxious morning in the canyon. When the Comanche had brought Jessie forward to trade, Ki had found it most difficult to remain hidden in the trees. If the Comanchero leader had taken her, Ki would have gone into the camp in broad daylight to rescue her, trusting on his *ninja* skills and his *karma*. But Jessie had been traded to the young man who had opposed the giant and gotten his trigger finger lopped off. Ki knew that he was a cut far above the other men and that Jessie would not be violated or mistreated. Besides, Ki could see that she was very ill from the discolored arm. She had been snakebit, and was in no condition to be carried away. So Ki knew that he could not deliver Jessie and the other women out of Comanchero Canyon this night as planned.

For the rest of that day he had made arrow shafts. He had selected straight branches from the pines and whittled them until they were smooth and straight. He had wetted the feathers of the arrows and then removed them from the broken shafts and made a glue to attach them to the new shafts. The arrows were not equal to those which had been broken, but when they were finished at sunset he went deep into the forest and tested them.

For a samurai, aiming was almost entirely the work of mental imagery. He located a target, visualized hitting that target and then drew back his bow and loosed an arrow. The Japanese bow turned a complete one hundred and eighty degrees around in Ki's left hand so that it pointed at his chest. Ki's new, untested arrows all streaked true to their target and Ki was satisfied after a few minute refinements.

Ki waited only until twilight fell upon the canyon, and then he moved into the camp. In a way, it was a much safer invasion because the dogs thought nothing of a human being moving about at that hour. Ki stayed in the deepest shadows and advanced on Trevor Morgan's cabin in spurts and starts that brought him in close. But Morgan was waiting on the front porch. Ki frowned. What was Morgan, friend or enemy? Had Jessie explained the circumstances to him, or was he hoping to capture the samurai and regain favor with the Comanchero leader? Ki simply did not know, and he could not afford to trust the man until he was very certain of his intentions.

So Ki slung his bow over his shoulder and moved across the camp very carefully. He circled behind Morgan's cabin and was disappointed to find that there were no doors or windows except the ones in front being guarded. The samurai edged along the wall. There was not much chance of being heard, for the camp was full of the sounds of men shouting and drinking and the occasional cry of a woman's voice.

Ki reached the corner of the cabin and slowly flattened against the wall to peer around its corner. The Comanchero was less than ten feet away, smoking a cigarillo. Now and then, someone would come staggering past his cabin and say something, usually about his new dying woman or his missing finger. Morgan would just keep smoking and waiting.

An hour passed. A dog trotted by within twenty feet of the samurai but either did not see Ki or wisely decided to mind its own business. A Comanchero and a woman, both drunk and loud, collapsed somewhere in the darkness and then coupled in the dirt. An owl swept across the face of the moon on silent wings and headed for the meadow to hunt field mice. Morgan finished his cigarillo, urinated off his porch and then got a glass and a bottle of whiskey. He poured the whiskey sparingly and sipped it for a while before lighting another cigarillo, leaning back against the cabin wall and humming a tune to himself.

Ki decided that he could not wait any longer. He had to see Jessie at once and decide about the Comanchero women as well as set a new time for their escape. The samurai inwardly stilled himself and moved forward. He slipped around the corner as quietly as a cobra, and his movement was so fluid and silent that he passed the window before the Comanchero even sensed something was amiss. The cigarillo was on its way up to Morgan's lips when he turned to see Ki only five feet to his left. He reached for a gun that he had hidden in his pocket but his hand did not even touch the weapon before Ki's foot came punching forward in a perfectly timed foot-strike that caught Morgan just below the ear and slammed him unconscious against the cabin. Before he even quivered, Ki grabbed him and hauled him through the front door.

"Jessie!" His first impression of her was that she was dead. She looked so pale and still that he felt sure that the poison had killed her. But he jumped forward and touched her neck. When he felt the slow, steady beat of her pulse, he expelled a deep sigh of relief. Ki turned, walked back across the room and closed the front door before he returned to Jessie's side.

"Jessie," he said again, kneeling down beside her. He touched her bruised cheeks and examined the terribly swollen and discolored arm. The wound itself was wrapped and when he undid the bandages, he found a green, smelly poultice. Ki set it aside and examined the fang marks. He raged inwardly for allowing such a thing to happen before he reset the poultice and rewound the bandages.

"Wake up," he whispered, softly.

She opened her eyes. "Ki, I *knew* you'd come soon. What about Trevor? I hope you didn't hurt him."

The samurai shrugged. "He tried to shoot me."

"That's my fault," she said. "I made the mistake of bragging a little about your *ninja* skill and he must have felt challenged. I'm sure that he would have brought you in to me at gunpoint just to prove his point."

Ki was not quite sure he understood this. Why should the Comanchero have to prove anything? He was obviously brave, because they had both seen him oppose the giant without support from a single one of over a hundred other Comancheros. To the samurai, Morgan's actions seemed illogical and very dangerous. Pulling a gun on a man could get you killed.

"Jessie, we need to talk. I was supposed to meet the Comanchero women tonight and lead them out of the canyon after catching us some horses."

"I know. Trevor told me the plan."

"Then what—"

"There are only two Comanchero women who dare to escape right now," Jessie explained. "One is named Juanita, and the other is Gloria Morales. Gloria is the beautiful girl we saw who was whipped."

"She is the giant's woman."

"Yes," Jessie replied. "And they think that the escape is off."

"It *is* off."

"No," Jessie said. "I want you to take them away tonight."

Ki had never argued with Jessie, never hesitated to do her will no matter how great the risks. Now, for the first time, he balked. "But I can't leave you," he protested. "I have pledged to protect you with my life and . . ."

Jessie saw how deeply the samurai was opposed to her wishes, but she had given the matter a great deal of thought and it seemed to her that there was no other way. "Listen, Ki. Nothing will happen to me here. I am safe, and besides, I won't be fit to leave this place on the run for quite some time. I know that, though it hurts to admit the truth."

"But we can all wait!"

"No," she said firmly. "You see, Gloria Morales is in great danger. Trevor has told me she wants to kill Hector Oxman. He thinks that she will if she cannot escape tonight. And of course, if she does, she is a dead woman."

The samurai stood up quickly. "But you might also die if I go away with them! I could not hope to return before the month ends. And if we have trouble, I might not be able to return to you at all."

"I've thought about that too," Jessie admitted. "But Trevor has agreed to help me escape and I somehow know he is a man of his word. He hates Oxman and is weary of the killing and torture. So, no matter what, I would be safe."

The samurai heard Jessie, but he was not ready to believe her. Trevor Morgan was brave, but he was no samurai, and Ki was not happy about leaving Jessie's fate in his hands.

Jessie could read his troubled thoughts. "Ki, I know you're deeply concerned about my welfare. But I will stay here in this cabin while I regain my health. I'm sure you will return in plenty of time with help, and we can clean this entire canyon out and free all the women. It is the best way, believe me."

Ki had never faced a request from Jessie that was any more difficult for him to accept. And yet accept he must, for he was honor bound to do so and her plan was sound and logical. He bowed his head. "I will do as you want," he said quietly. "But if any more dangers befall you, I—"

Jessie reached up and closed his lips with her fingertips. "Shhh," she said. "I promise to wait here for your return. Then we will all leave together. Once the other Comanchero women see that Gloria Morales and Juanita have safely escaped this canyon, they will begin to realize that it is possible. They will be ready to come out with us."

Ki stood up. He looked over at the still figure of Trevor Morgan lying unconscious on the swept dirt floor. "Are you sure, Jessie?"

She followed his gaze. Trevor was going to be furious when he revived, furious at himself, but even more so at the samurai. "You had better go and take the women before he awakens."

Ki nodded. "I know that Gloria is with the giant, but where is the one named Juanita?"

"I don't know," Jessie admitted. "You will have to ask Gloria. Good luck, my friend. Until we meet again."

Jessie looked so small and helpless that Ki felt desolated to abandon her. "Here," he said, slipping his knife and its sheath out from behind his waistband. "I insist that you take this."

"But you might need it yourself, and—"

"Please," he said. "I have never asked anything of you before. They would see a gun, but not the knife."

Seeing how much it meant to Ki, Jessie took the knife and slipped it under her blanket. "I will carry it with me at all times," she promised. "And when we are together again, I will trade it back to you for a gun."

"Agreed."

Ki turned and left without looking back, because that was the easiest way. He stepped over the still form of Trevor Morgan and left by the front door. He was thinking only of Jessica Starbuck, but knew that that would have to change in a hurry.

*I must enter the lion's den now,* he thought, remembering the size and strength of Hector Oxman. *And I must defang him and steal his woman.*

# Chapter 8

Ki knew exactly what had to be done before this night was over, and his only concern was for Jessie, whom he must leave behind, and for the pair of Comanchero women that he would take from this canyon. The Comanchero leader, Oxman, lived in the biggest of the cabins that were loosely clustered on an acre of ground. There was nothing uniform about the cabins, they faced all directions, and many were no more than rough pine shacks. But Oxman's cabin, because of his status, seemed to be situated about in the center of the camp, and it was definitely the most imposing structure in Comanchero Canyon.

The hour was growing late, and Ki knew that there was much to do before dawn. He had not only to free the two women and steal the horses, but take out the guards to the canyon and put some distance between himself and the pursuit that would come as inevitably as sunrise. Overhead, a cloud floated across the moon, and Ki took that as a good omen while he moved swiftly toward Oxman's cabin. There were some Comancheros still up and about, but he skillfully blended into the shadows of the night long before there was any real danger.

Ki expected that a man like Hector Oxman would have

many enemies who would welcome the chance to take his place. That meant that Oxman's cabin might be guarded, and so Ki approached it very cautiously. It was well that he did, for tied to the front porch was a huge and ferocious dog that had the appearance of being at least half wolf. Ki frowned and considered the paucity of his remaining choices. He could either use a *shuriken* blade to kill the beast instantly, or he could skirt the cabin and hope for a back door or window that could be forced open. He did not want to kill the wolf-dog except as a last resort, so he started to move around the cabin. But he checked himself, realizing he had a third, superior option.

With a smile, he drew the "cleaver" arrowhead from his quiver and nocked it to his bowstring. The wolf-dog saw Ki as he approached silently to within thirty feet of the cabin. A low growl sounded in its throat and the hair on its back lifted as the animal strained on its tether. Ki halted, drew his bow, and with nothing more than the moonlight to guide him, he sent the cleaver arrow flashing. It severed the rope and the dog, suddenly freed, lunged forward with a low rumble in its throat. As the dog leaped, the samurai moved aside and brought his hand slashing down in a perfectly timed *tegatana* blow. The iron-hard edge of his hand caught the savage dog at the nape of its neck. Had Ki not purposefully held back power, the neck would have been broken like a twig. But instead, the blow succeeded in slamming the animal to the dirt. Dazed, it still managed a low growl. Ki knelt beside the animal and smoothed its thick ruff.

"Do not be ashamed," he said, "for you have been taught wrongly and I understand. You are brave and only doing what you have been trained to do. If you want, you may come away with us."

The dog lay still, yet unable to rise because the blow had pinched the nerves in its neck. But it continued to growl, and Ki guessed that the animal had been badly mistreated to have so much hatred inside its great body. Ki stroked the wolf-dog once more, and the growling stopped. He left the stunned animal and moved to the cabin. The moon was high, and it bathed the camp in a soft, yellow light.

The door was locked from the inside, and Ki reached for his *tanto* blade before remembering that he had given it to Jessie for her protection. He pressed against the door and felt it give a little under his weight. He pushed harder, and then, suddenly, the door flew open and he found himself crashing headlong onto the cabin's rough wooden floor.

A yellow shaft of moonlight revealed Gloria Morales with her back to the far wall of the cabin. She was gagged and her wrists were tied behind her back. She was also naked, but Ki did not have time to appreciate the fact. With a roar, Oxman slammed the door shut, plunging the interior of the cabin into almost total darkness. He jumped forward with an upraised knife clenched in his massive fist. The man's weight bore Ki down, and when Oxman jerked back his chin, Ki knew the Comanchero was about to slit his throat. Ki tried to buck the Comanchero off and roll, but the man must have weighed three hundred pounds.

Gloria had seen the upraised knife too, and she realized that Ki was a dead man unless she gave him a fighting chance. So she threw herself blindly forward, and even though her hands were tied, she used her sleek but strong body to knock Oxman off balance.

Oxman cursed and clawed at Gloria. He dug his fingernails into her body and threw her aside like a sack of dirty laundry. She struck the inside of the door and was knocked unconscious. But her action had given Ki the momentary distraction that he needed, and he used it well. The fingers of his hand went as rigid as the tines of a pitchfork, and he drove them upward into the man's face. He missed the eyes but caught a nostril and snapped the giant's head back. With a cry of battle, Ki sent his other fist flashing toward the giant's throat. But Oxman was expecting that. He blocked the punch and slashed Ki across the chest. The samurai felt searing pain, but before Oxman could strike again with even more damaging effect, Ki grabbed his wrist and tried to hold the knife away. But his strength could not match Oxman's. As the knife came steadily downward, Ki kicked upward with his feet, then locked his heels around Oxman's face and yanked him over backward. The giant roared and, in the darkness, the two men threw themselves at each other.

Ki knew he was in a battle for his life—one that he very likely could not win. Oxman had all the advantages. The huge Comanchero was in familiar surroundings, and he had a knife. Furthermore, the area was so small and dark that it gave the samurai no opportunity to use his quickness and techniques. So when the two closed together Ki was thrown down again by the far heavier and more powerful opponent. This time, however, Ki managed to roll the giant, and they crashed over and over through furniture.

The samurai felt as if he were wrestling a grizzly bear. The man's strength was beyond belief! He would have given the great *sumo* wrestlers of Japan a battle for pure strength and ferocity. Ki had a hold of his wrist, and it was all he could do to keep the knife from slashing him again or plunging into his body. The man had a forearm across Ki's throat, and was slowly choking the life out of him. Ki struggled desperately to kick upward and use his heels in Oxman's face, but the giant would not allow the same trick to be used twice. He kept his massive head low, and the knife again began to edge downward toward Ki's body. This time Ki was not sure that he could stop it.

The door flew open and Ki rolled his head sideways to

see that Gloria Morales had regained consciousness. "Help me!" Ki grunted, not giving a damn about humility.

Since her wrists were bound tightly, she did the only thing she could think to do—bring her foot upward in a sweeping kick. The powerful blow caught Oxman under the chin and snapped his head back.

"I'll kill you for that!" he raged.

In answer, Gloria kicked him again in the small of his back. The giant winced in pain, and the woman kicked him right in the kidneys.

Almost immediately, Ki could feel Oxman weakening. Gloria kept kicking him in the kidneys, and every time her foot landed the giant trembled and shuddered like a big tree taking an ax-blow.

"Don't stop!" Ki grunted, having all he could do just to keep the knife up and away from his body. "Kick him harder!"

Gloria was kicking the Comanchero leader crazily. And they were powerful kicks! Suddenly, Ki twisted his body and the giant toppled over. Ki used a *migi-shotei* blow, catching the giant just below the ear. It should have finished him, but the giant thrashed wildly and Ki had to strike him two more times before he finally collapsed and lay still.

Ki climbed weakly to his feet. He spotted a candle and a box of matches, and he lit them before he closed the door again. Then he staggered over to the girl, who was still kicking the Comanchero leader. Even though she was gagged, she was making terrible sounds in her throat, and Ki pulled her away from the unconscious man.

"Stop it," he ordered, shaking her roughly. "He's finished."

The girl seemed to snap out of her rage. Then she bowed her head. Ki pulled the gag from her mouth and listened to her sobs of rage as he untied her wrists. Last night, they had already been badly chafed and discolored; tonight, they were bloody.

The girl reached for the Comanchero's knife, and Ki had to pull her away or she would have murdered him.

"Let go of me!" she spat. "He deserves to die a hundred times."

But Ki hung on. "Yes, I know that, but you have suffered too much already because of him. If you killed him while he was helpless, he would haunt you for the rest of your life. It is bad luck to kill a sleeping enemy."

"I don't believe in luck, good or bad," she said angrily. "And I don't understand why you came here for me. The woman you spoke of is too sick to leave this valley."

"She made me promise to take you and another named Juanita away. I will come back."

"She wants you to go without her?" Gloria did not seem to believe her ears.

"Yes," the samurai said. "She promised that she would wait for me to bring enough men to wipe out the Comancheros."

Gloria walked over and climbed into her shabby little dress. "I don't know why I'm telling you this, but your friend will be dead long before you can return."

"There is no time to argue," Ki said. "Get weapons and come show me where this Juanita sleeps so that we can go."

Gloria stared at him with her head cocked slightly to one side. She looked from the samurai to the unconscious leader. "You did it again, didn't you? You actually came back and did what you said you'd do."

Ki looked about the cabin. It was in a complete disarray, with clothes and supplies strewn about everywhere. Ki saw the giant's holster and gun hanging off a bedpost. He took the weapon and gave it to the girl. "You may need this before you are safe again."

Gloria took the weapon. "I will need it to blow my own brains out before they lay their hands on me again," she said quietly. "If I go with you now, there is no coming back for me. I will die first."

"Then we will *both* die," he said impatiently.

Gloria nodded. "Yes, we will both die; but at least it will be *our* choice and not his."

Ki saw the hatred in this girl as she looked down at the unconscious man. For a moment, he thought that Gloria Morales was going to shoot the giant, and the samurai almost jumped for the gun, for the noise of a shot would have ruined everything. But Gloria seemed to pull herself under control. A moment later, she was grabbing a rifle and a bandolier of cartridges. "I'm ready," she told him.

She followed him outside and the wolf-dog was still there, only now he was standing and watching the samurai with calm interest. When he saw Gloria Morales, his tail actually wagged, and when they hurried off to find Juanita, the big dog followed them.

Juanita Escobar lay away beside a Comanchero whose name was Daggett. Juanita did not know if that was his first or his last name. She did not know how old he was or anything of his past. All she knew was that he was one of the Comanchero lieutenants and that most of the men in this valley gave him a wide berth. Daggett was a very quiet man. He fed her well enough and beat her less often than most, but she lived in perpetual fear of the Comanchero, for it was common knowledge that he had a savage temper. The last woman he had kept had provoked him, and he had killed her with his bare hands. Daggett never smiled, never said much of anything. He was tall and thin, and his face was pocked. He bathed once a week and allowed Juanita to do the same. He wore a gun low on his hip and another one in the top of his right boot.

Now, as Juanita lay beside him, she dozed fitfully and

wondered about her family in Mexico, whether her mother was still alive. She had not been in good health when the Comancheros had come through their village. They had killed her father and taken Juanita with them. That had left Miguel, Jose, Rubenita, and Ignacio to help their mother through her grief. But they were still young, and the fields were rocky and hot. Juanita wondered if her family had starved. Then she reminded herself that in a small Mexican village people shared their joys as well as their sorrows and their food. Juanita kept that memory, and it gave her hope. There were days, even weeks, when just holding onto a little hope seemed impossible.

*"Pssst!"*

Juanita stiffened on the bed, and her large brown eyes opened in the darkness.

*"Pssst!"* The samurai appeared at the foot of the bed as if in a dream.

Juanita stared at the man. Her heart began to pound. He *had* come tonight after all!

She eased herself off the bed. In her haste to grab her clothes, she accidentally knocked over the unlit kerosene lamp that rested on an empty box beside her bed. The lamp crashed loudly and Juanita cried out in warning, for Daggett always slept within reach of a gun.

Ki did not see the sixgun but he sensed the Comanchero's movement, and he attacked the man without hesitation. His hand chopped down twice and Daggett lay still. Ki lit a match, glanced at the pale young Mexican woman and said, "Get dressed and take his gun. We are leaving."

Juanita nodded. There was no turning back now. Like Gloria, she knew that she had burned her bridges, and that death was the only possible result if this escape ended in failure. Her eyes met those of Gloria, and the two women seemed to exchange a silent message.

Gloria said, "Señor Ki is a man of great courage and

resourcefulness. We will have a fighting chance, Juanita."

"But what about the white woman that—"

"We can talk about it later," Ki said abruptly. "There is no time to do it now. I need a rope to make bridles and reins."

"I can do even better than that," Juanita said.

She quickly found him three bridles, bits, and reins that were stored under their bed. She also took a Mexican quirt and a braided reata and Ki was impressed with her ability to think well under the circumstances. A rope was a good thing to have for many reasons. Ki stepped outside, retrieved his bow and arrows, and they left—the samurai, the two Comanchero women, and the wolf-dog.

It was not difficult getting out of the camp, and once in the open they ran down the canyon until they reached the horses. Ki found Jessie's palomino and considered whether or not to take the swift animal. He had never ridden Sun, yet he knew that it trusted him and would carry him safely all the way to Circle Star if asked. And Gloria could ride his own pinto which was also a superior animal. But what about Juanita? Their pace would be dictated by the slowest horse of the three, and there was a clear drop-off in quality even though the Comanchero horses were all good animals.

Ki decided to take Jessie's palomino, knowing that she would want him to do so. And if they were overtaken he and Juanita could switch mounts, and then he would stay behind and delay their pursuers.

"Here," Ki said to the Comanchero women, "bridle these horses and lead them into those trees while I take care of the guards."

"But how?" Gloria exclaimed. "There are up in a small cave on the side of that cliff."

"I know that," Ki said. "Just do as I say!"

Gloria's dark eyes flashed, but Ki did not care. If they

had any chance of making it back to Circle Star, both these women were going to have to obey his every order without question. He was sure that Juanita would behave, but he was not at all certain about Gloria Morales.

Ki took his bow and headed down the canyon toward the entrance and the guards. In sharp contrast to the previous night, this one was pleasant. There was a good deal of moonlight to show him the way. When he came to within fifty yards of the entrance, he stopped in the shadow of some big rocks and selected an arrow. He knew that it woud be very difficult—if not actually impossible—to kill both guards before one of them fired a warning shot. If they had been accessible...But what was the good of thinking about that? Ki could see that they had pulled the rope ladder up behind them and that there was no chance of scaling the fifteen feet of smooth rock before being seen.

He nocked the arrow and waited for a man to show himself. He did not have to wait long. Presently, a guard stepped up to the edge of his lair and gazed out toward the Comanchero camp. Ki heard him say, "I wish there was some way to get into Oxman's woman. Just once, so I—"

Ki drew back his bowstring. Then his arrow jumped off the bowstring and streaked silently upward to thud into the guard's chest. The man's hands fluttered upward, and without a sound he pitched head first out of the rock cavern. His body made one complete somersault before it struck the valley floor with a heavy thumping sound.

The second guard yelled, "Ernie!"

For an instant, the second guard revealed himself as no more than a shadow in the dim interior of the cavern. Ki used that instant to its best possible advantage. He sent a second arrow flashing in the moonlight. It actually had to enter the cavern itself, and it almost seemed like a live thing as it probed the darkness and found its human target.

105

Ki heard a groan and then the sound of a body striking something hard.

He whirled and raced back to the horses. Slinging his bow and quiver over his shoulder, he took the palomino's reins. "I didn't have a clear shot at the second man. I don't know if he's dead or just wounded. Juanita, you take the Comancheros' horse. Gloria, you take my pinto."

They did not argue this time. The women had all three horses bridled, and the sleek animals quivered with excitement.

"Without making any more noise than possible, let's drive the entire herd out of this canyon and run them as far as we can before they scatter!" Ki said, grabbing a fistful of mane and swinging up onto Sun's back.

Neither the horses nor the women who rode them needed any further urging. They all jumped forward and burst into the herd of Comanchero horses, with the great wolf-dog seeming to do more than all three riders together. The big band was easy to start running. It took less than two minutes before Ki and the women had the animals streaming across the grassy canyon floor toward the cleft in the rocks. They reined in and allowed the big herd to funnel out of the canyon.

"I can't believe we're actually doing this!" Gloria cried, "It's—"

She didn't have a chance to finish. A rifle shot thundered from up above and Gloria Morales was flung from the pinto as if by an invisible hand. Ki used his knees and heels to drive Sun forward and shield Gloria. He jumped from the horse and drew an arrow. A second rifle shot flashed. Then the bow was in Ki's fist again, and another arrow was loosed upward. Like a heat-guided missile, it homed in on the muzzle-flash and found its target. The Comanchero guard screamed and his body tumbled headlong from the cavern to land not thirty yards from where Ki

106

now knelt beside Gloria, who lay pale and gasping in the moonlight. Beside her, the wolf-dog whined softly.

Ki saw the wound in her shoulder. It was ugly, but it would not ordinarily be fatal. She opened her eyes. They were wet with tears. Ki thought that she was crying from the pain, but he was wrong. "Now I can't go," she said. "So I want you to kill me."

"No," Ki said quietly. "You're a brave and a beautiful woman. They won't kill you."

"You don't understand. I won't live a day when Oxman gets a hold of me! He knows that I helped you."

Ki listened to the dying echo of the rifle shots. He could already hear shouts from the Comanchero camp, which was less than two miles away. There was so little time. But leaving this woman here, like this . . . *First Jessie, now this one,* the samurai thought miserably. It was very, very hard. And yet there was no decision to be made. The Comancheros would soon be upon them, and they would seize both him and Juanita and then torture them to death.

Ki looked up at Juanita. "Ride," he said. "I'll be along in a minute. Go!"

"We will come back for you and Miss Starbuck," Juanita cried. "Please, Gloria, believe in us. You are too smart for Oxman. He cannot let anyone know that you helped the samurai. *It would make him lose face!* So have faith in us, my friend. And wait!"

Gloria Morales looked up at her friend. Even though she was racked with the pain of a whipping and now a bullet, she seemed to realize that Juanita's words made sense. Hector Oxman *would* lose face if it became known that his own woman had betrayed him and the entire Comanchero camp. "All right," she said quietly, "I will do as you say and wait for your return."

While Ki tore his own clothes and used the cloth strips

to staunch the flow of her blood, she gripped his wrist and said, "When you come, we will be ready."

"I'll come," the samurai promised. "Nothing but death could stop me, and it is not yet my time to die."

"Then go!" she whispered urgently. "All our hopes depend on you and Juanita getting away safely."

Ki picked up the wounded Spanish girl and carried her into the rocks. "Try to wait until you see Trevor Morgan, for he will save you from the others. Then tell everyone that you were taken as my hostage. *This* will prove your words to be true."

Ki bound her wrists together so that it looked as if she had been a hostage. Then he raced back to Sun, leaped onto the animal's back, and galloped away with the wolf-dog on his heels.

Outside the hidden canyon, the land was sagebrush again, dry and hostile. Ahead of him, he could see the Mexican señorita riding with her heels locked tightly against the barrel of the pinto. So far she had managed to keep the Comanchero horses running in a closely knit bunch. But all those fine horses would soon scatter in this rough country, and very likely many would even turn back toward the grass and water of Comanchero Canyon.

And there were the Comanche to consider. They were still in possession of their best horses, and even though they were at the far end of the canyon and would not be as quick to take up the chase, they would be fearful pursuers.

Ki watched the Mexican girl ride. She was just a fair horsewoman, though he knew that her pluck and determination would make up for much of her lack of horsemanship.

Exactly how far was it to Circle Star? he wondered. How many minutes before the Comanche would burst out of their canyon and come after them? Five? Fifteen? And where was the next water and the *next* band of Comanche he had every reason to expect they might come across before reaching safety? And, finally, what had happened to Ed Wright and what remained of the Circle Star cowboys?

# Chapter 9

Even though it was late afternoon, Ed Wright dozed off and was immediately gripped in a terrible nightmare. Only it wasn't a nightmare, it was reality; when he rolled over and looked across the sage, he saw that the band of raiding Kiowa were still waiting to attack at sundown.

Two days earlier, the drought-stricken Texas Panhandle country had seemed to undulate under the merciless summer sky. A single huge cloud billowed up into the northeastern sky; but it teased the land, for it held no moisture, only wind.

He and the Starbuck cowboys had had little warning of the storm. One minute they were sweating and the air was still, the very next it was as if a Texas cyclone had risen out of the parched earth and hurled itself into their faces.

"Dust storm!" Ed yelled, grabbing his bandanna and pulling it up to cover his nose and mouth.

Cowboys hated dust devils and dust storms almost as bad as scorpions in their boots at sunrise. A dust storm blinded you and your horse, and if it was powerful enough it could drive weeds, stickers, and sand through your eyelids and blind you for keeps. There was nothing to do but grab your saddlehorn and hope your horse had enough sense to lower its head and stand stock-still until the storm passed.

But horses generally became terrified in a dust or sand storm. They tried to turn tail to it only to find that there was no set direction to avoid. Some horses began to whirl and others to buck. A few just went daffy and ran blindly into the storm, which was a pretty sure way for a cowboy to end up in a disastrous wreck. Ed's horse, a young but promising buckskin gelding, had chosen the latter alternative, and had taken off running. The Circle Star foreman had tried to stop the animal, but it had grabbed the bit in its teeth and raced on despite all the expert horseman could do under the poor circumstances.

Their downfall had occurred within two miles of where the storm had struck. The buckskin had stepped into a hole, and its foreleg had snapped like a dry branch. It was the most dreaded sound a cowboy ever heard, and every veteran had heard it more than a few times.

The Circle Star foreman let go and tried to kick out of his stirrups but the buckskin flipped over completely and crashed down on his legs. Ed felt a terrible pain shoot up through his body, and he almost lost consciousness as the gelding screamed and began to thrash. The foreman knew that one solid hoof blow in the temple could kill him instantly. With a supreme effort, he managed to drag his gun out of its holster and fire two shots into the gelding's head. The animal sighed, and its body jerked a couple of times before it died, pinning him solidly to the earth.

"Help!" he cried hoarsely into the raging wind. "Help!"

But he knew help would not come until the storm passed and the air cleared.

When his cowboys found him, both of his legs were so badly bruised that Ed couldn't put his weight on them, so they had to lift him up into the saddle behind George Beban. He and George rode double, but it was so painful

111

that the cowboys kept making signs all afternoon that they wanted to stop and rest the horses.

"They're plumb worn out," a cowboy said, though everyone knew it was the foreman who was in bad shape.

"We've got to catch up with Miss Starbuck," Ed told them, "but the storm has blown out the tracks."

The cowboy squinted at the horizon. "I don't know how to tell you this, boss, but it looks like we gonna get some rain."

And it *had* rained. Oh, God, how it had rained! And then any chance that they might have had of picking up Jessie and Ki's trail had been lost. They had ridden north for two more days. Their water was just about gone when they spied a couple of green-leafed trees up on a distant hillside.

"Water!"

The horses had not needed urging, either. And when they reached the life giving spring, Ed supposed that God hadn't abandoned them completely after all.

"We still got to find Jessie and Ki," he had vowed.

But then, he made that vow about five minutes before the Kiowa came loping their painted ponies over the eastern hill.

The Kiowa had rifles, and they attacked in full strength and without hesitation. There were at least thirty-five of them, and they were the very best of their kind, warriors who had dared to enter the land of their traditional enemy, the Comanche.

Ed had yelled to his pitiful collection of cowboys to take cover, but there really hadn't been much need for that. The trouble was, they were in an indefensible position and there was little cover except for the willows around the spring and two small trees that weren't even thick enough to hide one man.

The Kiowa were brave, and they knew that they could not afford to waste time with just a few cowboys. They were after Comanche women and Comanche horses, and the sound of a protracted gunfight dramatically reduced their chances of surprising their enemies.

In the first attack, they had come in so fast and furiously that they had overrun the cowboys and killed all but Ed, Danny Ortiz, Ron Eggler and Shorty McKay. But they had paid a dear price. Eight Kiowa were dead, and a few more were wishing they were dead and out of the fight. That left a dozen or so against four, and the Kiowa were getting cautious. A direct charge would have succeeded; but when it was done there wouldn't have been but a few living Kiowa to enjoy the fruits of their desperate victory.

"They're circling us again," Ed told his grim cowboys. "They'll come at us from out of a blinding sunset so that we can't hardly see them, and they'll sweep through here like the blade of a sickle."

"Then what can we do?" Danny Ortiz asked, his voice soft and Spanish.

Ed thought about that. As it was, they were bellied down in shallow holes like men already consigned to their graves. Ed didn't like the situation very well, and he glanced at the Circle Star horses tied to the trees. There were five horses that hadn't busted their reins and run away. Four cowboys and five horses sounded like lucky numbers to Ed.

"We can stay here and fight," he said, "or we can charge them like the cavalry."

The Circle Star cowboys looked at each other. It was Shorty McKay who said what they were all of a mind to do: "I don't reckon a cowboy can do much of anything off his horse except drink and screw women. And from what I seen, he don't do them things very good either."

The cowboys chuckled. That was Shorty, all right. He

was a man who could crack a joke neck-deep under an outhouse.

Shorty went on. "I consider myself to be a man who lives in the saddle, and I'd just rather die in one too. So if you're of the same opinion, I say we load all the lead beans in our sixguns and either live or die showin' them bloody Kiowa how a bunch of real *cowboys* can ride and fight on horseback."

"Suits me," Eggler said.

"Me too," Danny Ortiz added, looking to his foreman for the final okay. "Let's ride and get this thing over with."

Ed nodded. "Check your guns, boys. We won't have a second chance to reload, or even to use our rifles. It'll be just one pass through, and if there are any Indians left alive, then we turn and shoot their ponies. We can't expect to outrun 'em, and I'll be damned if I care to have a single one of them dogging our backtrail. So it's all or nothing."

"All or nothing," Shorty McKay echoed. "I like the sound of that just fine. Any man who rides away from this spring is going to be able to fill his canteen, and those of a lot of others."

The meaning was clear. All the Circle Star survivors looked over at their dead friends, knowing this had been the worst week in their entire lives. First they had lost their herd and wagons when the Comancheros had attacked and stampeded over their camp. And then they'd lost Jessie and Ki in a dust storm followed by a real gully-washer, and now these damned Kiowa had showed up and thinned their numbers even more. Lesser men would have wept, or been so stunned by this series of misfortune that they would be useless in a fight to the finish. But these men had taken the opposite reaction. The four that were left meant to see that at least one of them got back to Billy and Calvin at the wagons to tell the news of their further disasters. Somebody had to be told about Jessie and Ki's disappearance

114

and alert the army. It was the most important thing on their minds.

Ed glanced up at the sun. It would be setting in less than an hour, and he did not intend to allow it to get any lower and blind them. "Let's get this party started," he said when all the cowboys had checked and rechecked their weapons. "Let's show these heathen that a Circle Star cowboy is not a fella to be taken lightly. Now saying that, will one of you ugly galoots help me into the saddle?"

It was meant as a joke, talking about how tough they were in a fight and then having them witness the indignity of a cowboy being lifted up into the saddle. But the joke didn't play real well, and Ed wished he could climb onto his own horse, but his legs were so battered and swollen that he could not bend them at the knees.

So they lifted him into the saddle and the Kiowa began to whoop and holler as much out of curiosity as anything else. And when all the cowboys were mounted, the Indians probably expected their outnumbered quarry to cut and run. They'd have enjoyed that. Many a time an unwise white man had tried to outrun the Indians and found himself being stabbed and clubbed, prodded and spat upon, until he had not the strength to sit upright. He'd fall from his running horse and, if he were real lucky, he'd break his neck and die quickly.

Danny Ortiz was thinking about those same sorts of things. "Look at 'em!" he said. "They can hardly wait for the rabbit hunt to begin."

"Rabbit hell!" Ron Eggler spat. "What they got here is four goddamn *cougars!*"

Ed's mouth was set in a thin white line. He looked at all his men and figured he ought to say something about how proud he was of them, and how proud Jessie would have been too. But that would have made his three cowboys uncomfortable, so he just said, "You boys take care of yourselves."

And at that, he spurred his horse right for the Kiowa. They were mounted and ready, but the charge was so unexpected that they were taken completely off balance. Ed let out a wild Texas yell, and his cowboys did the same as they thundered ahead. He fired first, but was chagrined to see that he had managed only to blow a couple of feathers off the headdress of a Kiowa warrior. Who the hell could shoot accurately from the back of a running horse, anyway?

Beside him, Danny Ortiz fired next. His first bullet scored as a Kiowa brave threw up his feathered lance and rolled off his pony as gracefully as if he were trying to impress the living. Seeing that, the other cowboys took heart and opened fire in a volley that was impressive, given the fact that there was only four of them.

The Kiowa returned fire. They drove their heels into their ponies and came running. They were so expert on horseback that they guided their mounts with knee-pressure, thus freeing up both hands for the rifles that they favored over pistols.

Ed felt a storm of bullets whiz past his face. One buried itself into the rawhide-wrapped foundation of his old saddle, and another went through his horse's ear and then clipped him across the cheek. Ed heard Ron Eggler scream, and he just knew the cowboy was a goner and that they were only three now.

He shot twice more and killed one Indian and missed again. He waited a second and then laid aim on a big warrior with a purple jacket and red face-paint. When he pulled the trigger, the warrior straightened on his mount, but kept shooting. Ed fired again, and the big Indian kicked over backward and disappeared in the dust of his racing horse. Other Indians were going down as well. They

116

were within ten strides of the Kiowa, and there were only a half-dozen left on their horses. Ed took heart and emptied his sixgun and took out another one before he heard Shorty McKay grunt and yelp. Ed looked sideways to see the cowboy's death grin, and how he was trying to keep his gun up and working. But there was a crimson stain in the center of Shorty's chest, and he was shooting bullets downward into the sagebrush.

Danny Ortiz had always been lucky—with cards, with horses, and with wild, wild women. He was slim and handsome and dangerous, the best shot of the bunch, and now he was narrowing the odds in a hell of a big hurry. As Ed jammed his empty gun into his holster and reached for his rifle, he saw two more Kiowa rear up and then careen off their ponies and spill into the sage.

But Danny was out of bullets too, and it couldn't have happened at a worse time. They closed, and Ed saw that the Kiowa nearest to Danny was carrying a war club on a thong wrapped around his wrist.

Ed saw the Indian raise it to strike as Danny fumbled for his rifle. "Look out!" the Circle Star foreman shouted.

But the warning was too late. Danny raised his head just in time to take the stone club between his eyes. One minute he was in his saddle, eyes sparkling like jade; the next instant his face was a red mask and he was down.

Ed jerked his Winchester free and bailed off his horse, forgetting that his legs wouldn't support his weight. When he hit the ground, those legs buckled like wet newspaper and he rolled, feeling as if he were being swamped in a sea of pain. He tried to stand, but failed. So he fell forward and threw the butt of his rifle to his shoulder. There were only three Kiowa left to fight, and Ed allowed that he had an even chance. He was poor with a sixgun but right fair with a rifle, and he wiped the sweat from his eyes and took aim.

The remaining Kiowa should have pitched themselves off their racing horses and gotten down low and steady. But they were filled with blood-lust and a need to avenge their fallen comrades. So they charged, and Ed cut them down one by one. The last warrior did manage to hurl his lance, and its point buried itself in the dirt not an inch from Ed's side. But by then Ed was sending its owner to the happy hunting ground. The three riderless Indian ponies raced past him, and their hoofbeats thundered across the prairie, making the land echo. Ed stayed very still. He saw a wounded Indian and knew that the warrior would kill him in a moment. He considered the man as deadly as a shot rattler with the poison still dripping from its fangs.

"Shorty!" He took a deep breath and waited. "Ron!" No answer.

Ed wiped the sweat and grit from his face. The wounded Kiowa was crawling for a gun. Ed watched the Indian drag himself forward.

*What the hell am I going to do now?* he thought. *I can't even climb back onto a horse.*

The Kiowa brave reached the rifle he had been trying for, then levered a shell into its chamber. With agonizing slowness, the warrior twisted around, seeking to kill his white enemy. With great reluctance, and just before the Kiowa took aim, Ed shot him in the head. Then he began to crawl toward the spring and water. The horses would have to return to this waterhole. Ed figured to stay here until he could climb to his feet and mount one. That might be as early as tomorrow morning, or as much as three days from now. Maybe then he could gather up the other horses, both their own and the Kiowa ponies, and head for the place where they had lost their wagons.

Would Billy and Calvin still be there? Alive? Ed Wright did not know the answers to anything anymore. He had lost all but those two cowboys, and there was a good chance they were either dead or gone.

He pulled himself up to the spring, then dragged his useless legs to one of the trees, where he propped himself up with the rifle laid across his lap. *I've failed everyone*, he thought. *And I guess being the last man alive out here is the worst punishment of all.* Ed Wright gazed tiredly across the scene of battle and saw all the dead men, red and white—men mostly younger than himself, with more years to live, and more to lose in their dying. *What a goddamn awful waste*, he thought with an ache inside of him growing bigger and bigger.

The Circle Star foreman bowed his head to his thick forearm and began to cry. It was all right; there were no men left to set an example for.

# Chapter 10

Jessie heard the rifle shots echoing down Comanchero Canyon, and she knew that Ki had run into trouble. She sat up in the dark and reached for a match to light the kerosene lamp beside the bed.

Trevor Morgan reached it first. When the light flared, he studied Jessie. "It's that samurai of yours, isn't it?"

"Yes, along with Gloria Morales and a girl named Juanita."

Trevor's head snapped up. "Gloria too?"

"Yes."

"I should have guessed. I didn't help her escape, so she took the first offer that came along."

"Ki can get her out of there," Jessie said stubbornly.

They both heard men shouting, and then running horses. "It sounds to me as if your man didn't make it out of the canyon."

Jessie refused to believe that, even for a moment. "Ki is only human, but I'll bet he and the two women are running free right now."

"Yeah," Trevor conceded, a little sheepishly. "I guess I'm probably just jealous. Since I couldn't figure out a way, and the samurai did, I'm halfways eager to see him fail."

"You have to help us!" Jessie said hotly. "It doesn't matter who gets the glory or whatever you might call it. Their lives are at stake!"

"You're right," Trevor said. "Your man made me eat my words. I said that no one could get past me—but the samurai did. He hit me so fast I never even got a clear look at his face."

"He could just as easily have killed you," Jessie reminded the jealous young Comanchero. "And now he may be caught at the entrance to this canyon. I *have* to find out."

But when Jessie tried to rise off the bed, she found that the snake poison still had the effect of making her weak and feverish. She looked up at Trevor and saw him checking his gun. "What are you going to do?"

"I'm not sure," he confessed. "But if your samurai and Gloria Morales are pinned down by gunfire, when the Comanche overtake 'em, God Himself couldn't think of a way to save their lives."

"Try!" Jessie whispered urgently. "Try to do what you can for them."

He stopped at the doorway and turned back to face her. "You've already told me there will be no ransom or reward except for a cowboy's job. I'd say you're running a little short of incentives, lady."

"If they're pinned down in the entrance to this canyon and you help them, I'll up the ante," Jessie told him. "You can name your own price."

The smile on his handsome face widened. "I'll hold you to that, Miss Starbuck, and I almost hope your samurai and Gloria are trapped. It will give me a chance to pull off a miracle."

*  *  *

Trevor Morgan held his smile until he was out into the night. Then a grim line formed across his wide mouth and he started running. The camp was in a state of chaos. Comancheros were stumbling out of their cabins and tents half-dressed and half-asleep, with more than a few of them half-drunk. They were tucking in their shirts and cursing as they ran barefooted down the valley with their weapons clenched in their fists.

Comanche were galloping headlong through the camps, scattering men afoot like dry leaves in a high wind. Stripped to loincloths, holding their rifles, and with their long, black hair streaming behind, they passed Trevor moving like fingers of death to disappear down the valley. Trevor knew in his heart that he could not save the samurai from the Comanche. If Ki, Gloria, and Juanita were not through the canyon and running with a good two- or three-mile head start, they would be dead before dawn. He almost slowed to a walk because the mounted Indians made him realize fully that he was too late to change whatever happened or might yet happen this night.

But he was wrong. The samurai was gone and so was Juanita, but Gloria Morales was found hidden in the rocks with her hands tied. Where the hell was Hector Oxman! Trevor wondered, before he realized that the Comanchero giant would have also been incapacitated by the samurai.

*I hope they killed him,* Trevor said to himself, even as he yelled, "Hey, Ross, take it easy with her! Can't—" The blustery words died in his mouth. "She's been shot!"

"Goddamn right she has," Ross yelled. "But it won't save her pretty neck from what Hector will do to her for this."

Trevor moved over and grabbed Ross by the collar and jerked him completely off his feet. The man snarled and clawed for his gun. But Trevor was expecting the move,

122

and his own gun was already in his fist. "Try it," he whispered. "Try it and take a long-awaited one-way trip to hell."

Ross moved his gunhand away from his holster. "You might not be so lucky as to get the drop on me next time. And with that missing trigger finger, I don't suppose you'll have much of a chance when I put a bullet through your gizzard."

Trevor used his middle finger to pull the trigger of his pointed sixgun. The bullet passed right between Ross's spread legs. The man jumped back in fear. "You kill me, Oxman will skin you alive."

"He might already be dead," Trevor said. "Then what?"

Ross had no answer to that question. He was a lackey. Not that he was a coward, but he acted cowardly, and there *was* a difference. Ross never braced anyone unless he had all the odds in his favor. And when that occurred, he could be deadly. Trevor had seen him kill four Comancheros, each a shade faster with a gun than himself, and he had done it by using his brains. Catching his enemies when they were most unprepared, drunk, half asleep or so badly hung-over their hands shook. Trevor knew he had made himself a mortal enemy.

He picked Gloria Morales up and listened to the angry cursing of the Comancheros as they raced out of the canyon in a vain search for their horses. "You can plainly see that this girl was taken as a hostage and did not go of her own free will. Do you think she tied her own wrists together like this?"

Ross momentarily forgot about vengeance. He studied the leather thong that bound the girl's bloody wrists. "Well, maybe not. We'll get to the truth of it when we catch whoever shot Ernie and Claud with their goddamn arrows."

"Maybe Kiowa," Trevor said, looking at the two bodies.

"Kiowa, my ass!" Ross screamed. "No Indian uses an arrow like they got shot with. I don't know what the hell is going on, but those Comanche will have the sonofabitches who did this, and they'll bring them back alive for a reward. Then we'll have the answer to a lot of damn questions. Hey, where you taking her?"

"To the Kiowa medicine man," Trevor said.

"You better take her to Oxman and ask first."

"She might bleed to death first," Trevor said, looking down into the woman's face. "And Oxman would be mighty unhappy about that. Even with a hole in her shoulder, this girl is worth twice what any other woman in camp would fetch. You want to tell Oxman that you voted that his woman should bleed to death?"

Ross shook his head violently. He was whipped, and he knew it. "You better try to save her," he said in anger. "That woman has a powerful hold over Oxman. Never saw another who could match it. But if she betrayed him and he's dead, we'll roast her tomorrow."

But Trevor knew that already. As soon as he was out of hearing of the Comancheros, he said, "Can you hear me, Señorita Morales?"

She opened her eyes, and with the moonlight on her lovely face, her skin was very pale, and so translucent that he could see a blue vein throb near her forehead.

"Did they escape?" she whispered.

"Yes."

A slow smile transformed and relaxed her face. "He'll come back for us, Trevor Morgan. The samurai will make it, and he'll bring help. This canyon, it . . . it's finished."

"Don't say any more," he whispered. "Save your strength. I'm taking you to the Comanche medicine man. We'll get that bullet out of your arm and . . ." Trevor did not need to finish his explanation. The señorita had fainted from pain and loss of blood.

Jessie found the strength to walk to the door of Trevor's cabin. As the Comanchero approached, she said, "Bring her in here. I'll care for her."

"The Comanche medicine man will—"

Jessie's voice sharpened. "I know firsthand about his powers. I also know that he did not want to save me but only did so because Pale Horse threatened his life."

"Oh. I didn't realize that."

"Well, now that you do, please bring her into the cabin. You can boil some water and we'll see if we can get the bullet out before she awakens. It looks nasty."

"It is," Trevor said, his voice shaking with anger. "But Ki killed both Ernie and Claud, and he and Juanita are making their run."

Jessie followed them back into the cabin. "If we save her, can you keep Oxman from taking her back?"

"No," Trevor said. "He'll not want to admit she betrayed him, so he'll beat her to death, or starve her. He'll make it look like she died on her own."

Jessie watched Trevor lay the girl down gently on his bed. "This cabin of yours is becoming more like an infirmary every day."

"Yeah," Tevor said. "But tomorrow, Oxman will want her back."

Jessie waited a moment before she spoke. "Trevor, we simply can't let that happen."

"I know," he said. "I have to kill Oxman. It's the only chance that Gloria has for life. In his cabin and under his rule, she wouldn't last a week."

Jessie ripped open the young woman's dress and studied the bullet hole. "Get that water to boiling," she said. "This is going to be hard."

While the water was heating, Jessie washed the girl's

face, neck, and arms, then her shoulder. The bullet seemed to have gone under the shoulder bone, and when Jessie got Trevor to roll her over, she saw that the bullet had actually passed all the way through the young woman.

Trevor could not help but smile. "Now she has a good chance to make it," he said. But then he added quickly, "You don't think the bullet went through her lung, do you?"

"No," Jessie replied. "If it had, we'd hear the air escaping from the lung when she breathed. I think we're in luck. Ki stopped the bleeding in the front, but she lost a lot of blood from underneath. That's our main worry. That and getting the wound cleaned out and cauterized."

"Yeah," Trevor said. "But all that still don't take care of Oxman."

Jessie looked right into his eyes. "You said you were going to kill him before you left this canyon. The question I ask you is this—why not do it before he gets to her?"

Trevor nodded. This had been his own reasoning as well. "I have to wait until he calls for her. Then I'll face him. If I kill him now, the Comancheros will think that he died because of the girl, and then nothing will keep them from her."

"Do you stand any chance at all with that finger?" Jessie asked.

"Not really. Oxman is fast, despite his size and bluster. I might have outdrawn him before, but with this hand the way it is, I don't have much chance."

"Then—"

"There is no choice!" he blurted. "Not for Gloria, not for me. When he comes here to claim his woman, I'll have to step out and draw against him. That's all there is to it. Maybe I'll get real lucky and beat him."

"I think the water is boiling by now," Jessie said. "As for Oxman, we can face that after we take care of Gloria."

Trevor Morgan nodded and went to get the boiling water. When he returned he poured it into the bowl and watched Jessie tear a strip from her dress and begin to gently cleanse the bullet wound. "Look at your arm. It's still twice normal size. You should be a patient yourself, not doctoring someone else."

"Is that right? And who would take my place—you?"

"Maybe," he said, stung by her unexpected rebuke.

Jessie looked at him, realizing her words had been delivered more sharply than intended. "I'm sorry for snapping at you, Trevor. It's just that I'm worried about what happens when Oxman arrives."

Trevor tried to feign indifference. "I either kill him or he kills me."

"What if *I* killed him," Jessie said.

"You?"

"I've had to kill a good number of men to protect my own life and property. I take no pleasure in it, but neither would I lose sleep over the death of such an animal. Remember, I saw how he castrated a man, and what he did to your own back. I doubt that there is a man in Texas more deserving of death."

"There isn't," Trevor said. "But there are damn few harder to kill, either. Besides, if you killed him, they'd crucify you."

"And not you?" Jessie asked.

"No," he told her. "I'm one of them. Among the Comancheros, any man may challenge any other. It just has to be a stand-up fight. No bushwhacking. That's the rule that holds everyone in check. If one of us kills another without warning, he is sentenced to a slow death."

"I see," Jessie said with a frown. "That does make it more complicated, doesn't it."

Trevor nodded. "I *have* to win," he said. "If I don't, you both lose as well."

"Can you even draw your gun and fire without your trigger-finger? Show me."

"Now?"

"Yes. It can't take but a second."

Trevor stood up and faced a blank wall after emptying his weapon of bullets. His gunhand came to rest over the butt of his revolver, and he tensed, then made his play. His hand streaked downward, and the gun came up smooth and fast until he tried to pull the trigger. Then, there was a split-second's fumbling—enough to make the difference between living and dying.

Jessie eased Gloria over and began to bandage the wound. "You ever fan your gun?"

"Fanning the trigger is for showoffs and fools."

"Yes," Jessie said, "I know that. But at close range, it can still be accurate and very fast. You get Oxman to come right up to the porch, then you step out and make your play. I don't think you'll lose much—if any—speed."

A shadow of hope crossed his face. "That makes sense," he said in an excited voice. "I think you just might be absolutely right!"

Jessie nodded. "Help me finish this up. Then, you should practice a little. Not too much. But enough."

He frowned. "How come you know so much about gun-fighting, Miss Starbuck?"

Jessie thought of Longarm, who had once confided some secrets of the professional gunfighter, and told her about fanning. "I just keep my ears open," she said.

Trevor grinned. "If I get through Oxman, you're my woman until we get back to the big ranch of yours. Do you know what that means?"

"It means absolutely nothing."

Trevor laughed outright, and the sound of it was music to Jessie's ears. If a man could laugh before a gunfight, he had a real chance.

"Morgan! Morgan, goddamn you, I want my woman!"

Jessie got up and opened the door a crack. "It's Oxman, and he looks ready to go to war."

Trevor finished tying his gun down. Then he picked up his Stetson and put it firmly on his head. Looking at Jessie, he said, "What are you going to do if I lose?"

"You're not going to lose. You have to know that you can beat him this morning," she said. "If you don't believe it, you haven't any chance at all."

"All right," he said, "I believe it. You saw how fast I bring a gun out. And with the fanning, all I have to do is to get close so that accuracy doesn't matter. If he'll let me in close, I can beat him, Jessica."

"Of course you can," she told him before she reached up and kissed him full on the lips. "No matter what you've done in the past, and no matter what happens out there in the next few minutes, you're a good, decent man, Trevor Morgan."

"Write that on my grave marker as my epitaph," he said, easing her away from him.

Trevor pushed open the door. It was dawn. The canyon walls were still in shadow, but the sun was high enough that the huge form of Hector Oxman was plainly visible, standing about thirty paces away. Jessie stayed inside, though she could see everything once Trevor stepped off his porch. She knew that Trevor had to narrow the distance by at least half or he'd have no chance of hitting the Comanchero leader. Not fanning his gun, he wouldn't. Jessie glanced sideways to a case where he kept his weapons. On impulse, she grabbed one of Trevor's extra sixguns and made certain that it was loaded.

"That's far enough!" Oxman bellowed. "I want Gloria Morales!"

"She's inside," Trevor replied. "And I'm laying claim to her. From now on, she's *my* woman."

Hector laughed, but it was not a funny sound. "You already have the white woman with the copper hair! What's the matter, did she die of the snakebite already?"

"No, she lives," Trevor said. "But I want *both* of them."

The smile on Hector Oxman's face slipped badly. "I think I will kill you right now."

Jessie felt a sense of doom. Oxman was just not going to allow Trevor to close in on him. Jessie raised the pistol in her hand and took aim.

"Draw!" Oxman raged.

Trevor Morgan drew, and his gun came up fast and clean from its holster, as fast as did Oxman's. And when Jessie saw his left shoulder move to start the fanning motion, she pulled her trigger twice.

Three guns exploded almost simultaneously. Jessie's bullets punched twin holes in the Comanchero's chest, and Oxman's shot went wide. But Trevor was fanning his gun so fast that the shots blended together and he did not stop until his gun was empty.

Oxman pitched over dead and Jessie retreated deeper into the dim interior of the cabin.

It took Trevor a moment to realize that he had killed his hated enemy. Jessie watched him take a step backward. Then Trevor calmly expelled the spent cartridges from his smoking sixgun and reloaded. "Ross," he said, his head snapping up, "have you got any objections to calling me boss?"

The Comanchero had plenty of objections, but he swallowed them like sour milk. He stared at the gun in Trevor's fist and said, "No, boss, I reckon not."

Jessie relaxed. She moved over beside Gloria Morales and took her hand, hearing Trevor say, "Anyone else have any objections? Where's Daggett?"

130

Ross said, "He and some of the men are out catching up their horses. They want to go after whoever took Daggett's pretty señorita."

"From now on, *I* say who comes and goes, and when," Trevor proclaimed. "Now you men drag that carrion out of my sight!"

A minute later, Trevor stepped back into the cabin and slowly closed the door and leaned up against it with a sigh. He looked like a man who had just gotten his death sentence overturned as he was about to climb the gallows. "I really beat him," Trevor said, holding his gun up before his eyes. "I finally killed that animal!"

Jessie nodded. "I told you that you could do it if you believed—"

"But I *didn't* believe," he admitted in wonder. "I tried to, but when Oxman didn't let me come in on him, I figured I was the same as dead."

"Maybe you had a lucky shot."

"One shot wouldn't have stopped him," Trevor said, "not any more than a single pistol shot would stop a horse. No, I hit him twice dead center."

Jessie went to him. There was nothing in the world to be gained by confessing that it had been her two bullets that had killed the giant. Trevor Morgan was still brave and decent. The fact that he had stood and fought while not believing he had the remotest chance of winning made him even more special.

"What am I going to do now?" he asked. "I don't want to lead a raid on some poor village down in Mexico. But they'll be expecting me to."

Jessie took him into her arms. "Why don't we worry about that tomorrow?" she gently suggested, unbuckling his gunbelt, and tossing it aside as her hands came up behind his neck and drew his lips to her own.

His mind was so filled with the miracle of his victory

and survival that he did not respond for a moment. But then his arms enfolded her and she could feel his passion stirring.

He stepped back and began to unbutton his shirt. "I can't even offer you my bed, Jessica. There's a woman already in it."

"I know," she told him. "And before Gloria wakes up and catches us making love, we had better make the most of what little time we have."

The cabin was not so dim that Trevor could not see the proud fullness of Jessie's breasts and the narrow waist that rounded into her lovely hips. "Oh, my," he said. "I know I'll never have another chance at you, so I'm going to make the most of it."

Jessie found an extra blanket and spread it on the floor. "You're right," she told him as she watched him quickly undress.

He was already swollen with desire. When he covered her, she kept her legs together for another moment and whispered devilishly, "I promised you that you could name your own price if you saved our lives. Is *this* your price, Trevor Morgan?"

"It's the only price I care about right now," he said thickly.

Jessie spread her legs wide apart and reached down to grip his buttocks and pull him into her. "In that case, be my guest!"

He drove his stiff rod deep into her, and Jessie sighed with pleasure. He was careful not to touch her injured arm, but all the rest of her beautiful body was fair game. He moved powerfully in and out of her slick and ready womanhood. Jessie was an expert lover, and she used her body to milk him slowly at first, then faster and faster, until they both rose on a sea of passion that carried them ever higher. The new Comanchero leader covered her mouth with his own, and then their bodies locked and spasmed with an explosive climax that spiraled them away into the realm of heavenly insanity.

Afterward, he held her close and whispered, "All my life I would have wondered what it would be like, possessing a rich and beautiful lady like you, Jessica Starbuck. And if we ever get out of this mess alive and I go to work for you, I'll know how it feels to be inside you and not be driven half crazy by the wondering."

"I'm just a woman," she told him.

"No," he said with a firm shake of his head, "you're more than that. You're a beautiful love-goddess."

"And you're a *good* Comanchero, Trevor Morgan. The only good one I ever heard of. But we're going to bring these men down."

"Yeah," he said, "we're going to do that, all right."

On the bed, Gloria Morales stirred fitfully. Trevor lifted himself off Jessie and said, "I guess that was my one touch with paradise."

"No," she told him. "That woman on the bed could be the answer to your dreams, Trevor. Give her and yourself time. If everything goes as I hope, someday I'll be invited to your wedding."

Trevor reached down and pulled her to her feet. His voice sounded light and even gay when he spoke. "Given what we just did, I guess it's crazy to say this, but I hope you're right, Jessica. In fact, I *know* you're right."

# Chapter 11

From his vantage point by the hillside spring, Ed Wright could see what looked like a hundred miles to the west, east and south. And now, as he finished burying his fine young cowboys, he limped to his horses. He had decided to take three of his cowboys' saddles and mounts back to Circle Star, and so he had created a string by tying them head to tail. These were all good, fast horses, and Ed had loaded them with rifles, canteens, and the skin bags filled with water that the Comanche favored. The way Ed had it figured, even if he didn't find another drop of water between here and Circle Star, they could make it. And if they ran into Comanche or Kiowa, he had enough firepower to give them one hell of a good fight before they lifted his scalp.

Ed stood by the horses and studied the cowboys' graves. They were unmarked, and, in fact, he had taken great care to leave no sign of them. When Indians come through here again, they would see the bones of their dead and be mighty upset.

"Sleep well, compadres," he said, tipping his Stetson to the good men to whom he owed his life.

With a grunt of pain, he just managed to get his foot in

the stirrup and pull himself up into the saddle. It was an effort that left him sweating and shaken. Both of his legs were on the mend, but he sure wasn't ready to run any footraces yet. Ed spurred his mount and headed on down the hillside. He did so with a good deal of reluctance, for when a man was riding low country, he was at the mercy of anyone on a higher ridge.

Something caught his eye even before he was off the hillside. Ed drew his horse to a halt and squinted. Two riders were moving parallel to the way he was heading, and they were flying.

"Damn," the Circle Star foreman said. "I ain't even off this hillside and already I spot Indians."

He decided to wait until the pair passed out of sight. They were about two miles away, and he wondered why anyone would run that fast in this hot weather. They rode bareback, so they had to be Indians, but those two horses sure could cover ground. Palomino and . . . and a pinto.

"Jesus Christ!" Ed whispered. "That's Jessie and Ki!"

Ed was seized with joy. He spurred his horse into a headlong gallop that carried him down the hill. Far in the distance he saw a cloud of dust that told him why the pair were moving so fast. They were being chased, though with those two fast horses and that kind of lead, it seemed as if Jessie and Ki were as good as home. The Circle Star foreman pulled his gun and fired into the air.

Still two miles away, Ki twisted around and saw the horseman leading three saddled but riderless horses. It was still too far away to see who it was, but the samurai knew it was a cowboy by the cut of his hat and the way he rode.

"Who could that be?" Juanita yelled.

"I think it's Ed Wright," Ki decided out loud. "Come on, let's go see!"

When they came together, there were a hundred questions each man wanted to ask, but Ed only allowed himself one of them. "Where's Miss Starbuck?" he shouted, studying the barelegged Mexican girl who clung desperately to her racing horse's back.

"She's in Comanchero Canyon, and she's ill with a rattlesnake bite. She didn't have the strength to come out with us."

"So you left her?" Ed couldn't believe the samurai would do such a thing, but he obviously had.

Ki hid his irritation well, for he had been insulted. "This is Juanita. If I hadn't obeyed Jessie and brought her out, she was a dead woman. We're going to get some help and come on back."

Ed grunted his understanding. "Juanita," he said, struggling to dismount, "you look mighty grim riding bareback. Let's take a minute and get you a change of horseflesh and a saddle."

The girl nodded with relief. They stopped and Ki said, "We've been running since before daylight. Sun is about played out too. I think I'll relay onto a new horse."

"Take your pick," Ed told the samurai. "As you can see, I've got three fresh ones."

Ki recognized the horses, and he knew who had ridden them. "Are they dead?" he asked.

"Yeah," Ed told him. "Happened two days ago, just up on the hillside back yonder. Them and all the rest. They died well but too damn young. It should have been one of them come down to meet you instead of me."

Ki felt the man's pain. "Some things aren't ours to decide," he said.

Juanita looked back. The cloud of dust was chasing them and it was closing. She waited anxiously as Ed dismounted and shortened the stirrups of an empty saddle. "They're coming up quickly," she offered.

Ed didn't even turn around. "I reckon they are for a

fact," he said. "But don't you worry none. This is time well spent. If these stirrups are too long, you'll be crippled up in no time at all. This is rough country, and we are going to be covering it mighty fast. These stirrups have got to be right."

Juanita's head bobbed up and down. She looked at the horses and all the rifles that they carried. She saw the water, too, and some of the anxiety in her face disappeared. "They will have to catch us."

"And they can't," Ed told her. "These horses are better'n theirs—I think."

But Ki was not so sure. They had hundreds of miles to go before they reached Circle Star, and a lot of bad things could happen over that kind of distance. The Comanche knew this land. They would know shortcuts and how to pace their best horses in order to win this race of death.

And there was one other factor. They were all stronger horsemen than Juanita. She was the weak link, and Ki knew that her lack of riding skill would cost them precious minutes that could add up to a fatal showdown long before they reached safety.

He looked at Ed Wright. The man appeared to have aged ten years and become old. Maybe Ed wasn't up to the punishment they would have to endure to outlast the Indians. Ki shook the thought out of his head. The Circle Star foreman wasn't the man he used to be, but he was still mentally tough, and he could stay in the saddle as long as any Comanche warrior or Comanchero.

Ed finished with the stirrups. "Climb onto this fresh horse and let's see how these stirrups fit you."

Juanita tested them.

Ed rubbed his jaw. He was fussy about having things exactly right, and Ki knew that he thought he needed to shorten the stirrups just a little more. The samurai studied the approaching band of Comanche. They were flying.

"Ed," Ki said. "I think those stirrups will be good enough for now. Don't you agree, Juanita?"

The girl nodded vigorously. "Please, señores, let's ride!"

"I think she's got a good point," Ki said.

Ed shrugged his big shoulders. "All right, but if it starts to hurt at the knees, you just sing out and we'll take up a little more slack. Hear now?"

"Yes!"

Ed mounted with great difficulty. Ki wondered about his legs but did not want to spare the time to ask how he had been injured. So they waited until the foreman was up and well seated, and then they galloped south with a hot wind in their faces and three relay horses behind them.

Their lead was no longer comfortable but it *was* a lead, and Ki intended to lengthen it during this first night. That is, if the girl was able to stick in her saddle that long.

The day passed, but not slowly. Juanita was struggling gallantly to keep the pace, but she kept falling behind. Twice before sunset, she worried aloud that her horse was limping, but it clearly was not. Ki and Ed exchanged grim looks, for it was becoming very clear that the Mexican girl could not possibly ride all the way to Circle Star at the rate they were traveling. She might endure another full day in the saddle, but that would be the limit of her physical endurance.

Right at sunset, they halted and let the horses blow. The animals were wringing wet and covered with dust. They watered them sparingly and allowed them ten minutes to graze on the short bunchgrass, but Ki knew their bellies would still be almost empty.

While Juanita wetted a rag and bathed the raw insides of her thighs, Ed and Ki climbed a little rise of land and looked back at the cloud of dust that followed them.

"I think we've stretched our lead again," the Circle Star foreman said.

Ki agreed. "If we can keep the señorita in the saddle until daybreak, we can stretch it even more."

Ed glanced over his shoulder. "That's a big 'if,' my friend. It's not that she ain't trying to tough it out; but tryin' sometimes just isn't good enough."

Ki did not want to say so, but thought the foreman was right. "If we had some grease she could put to the insides of her legs, it would help."

Ed winked. "If she'd let us apply it, I reckon we'd come up with something, huh?"

Ki blushed. "You're younger inside than you look on the outside," he told the man. "How about some lather from between our own horses' legs?"

Ed thought about it. "Worth a try," he said. "If it works for a horse, I don't see why it wouldn't work for a human."

Ki went over to Sun and patted the palomino, then slipped around behind it and ran his fingers up where its legs joined. There was plenty of white lather. Not sure how to approach the subject, he walked over to Juanita and said, "Here. This might help a little. Can't hurt."

She studied the lather for a moment and then she smiled. "I will try it. She lifted her skirts to her knees just as casually as if she did such a thing every day. And maybe, Ki thought, she had been forced to do so in the Comanchero camp. At any rate, he watched her apply the horse's lather to the insides of her swollen and red calves. She had very slim and pretty legs, and he found himself wishing he could see more. But when she looked up directly into his eyes, he turned away while she anointed the inside of her thighs.

"You may turn around now, Señor Ki," she told him.

"How does it feel?"

"Wet and warm."

Ki blushed even deeper this time, and he moved away quickly. As he passed Ed, the older man was grinning.

But no one was grinning the next morning. It had been a long, dangerous night filled with difficulties. Clouds had blocked out the moonlight, and they had ridden blindly into ravines and arroyos. Ed had led the way, and he'd just allowed his horse to pick out the trail while the rest of them followed. Once, sometime around four or five in the morning, he'd grunted, "The Comanche will be making up ground on us tonight. They ride better in total darkness than white men."

"If that's true," Ki said, "then I should be leading because I'm not a white man."

"You want the damned lead, take it," Ed grunted.

But Ki had stayed back. He followed the girl, and he could see her silhouette and how her head kept falling down on her chest and then snapping up almost as if by reflex. The samurai knew that she could not go on for another twenty-four hours. Somehow, they would have to think of something, even if that something was tying her in the saddle while she slept. Only, that wouldn't work. There was just no way to support the upper body, and when it fell over, serious injury could and often did occur.

Daybreak was spectacular. The land seemed to fill with brilliant colors that flooded across the Texas Panhandle like warm honey over breakfast pancakes. Both Ed and Ki tried to cheer up the señorita and keep her awake. "Bet Old Mexico has sunrises the equal of this one every morning," Ed began.

Juanita said nothing. The insides of her legs, despite the horse lather, stung like burning nettles, but at least that pain kept her from falling asleep.

Ki said, "Where do you live?"

She roused herself to answer. "A little village called Candelaria."

"Beautiful name," Ki offered. "What does it mean in Spanish?"

"Candle mass. Yes, it is a lovely name, though it is a very poor village."

"Tell us about it," Ki said, twisting in his saddle to look back now that the light had grown bolder. What he saw confirmed Ed's bleak assessment. The Comanche and Comancheros were gaining on them. They were less than ten miles back, and Ki estimated that they numbered at least thirty riders. The thought occurred to him that should he and Ed lead them to Circle Star headquarters, their numbers might be great enough to annihilate every man on the ranch.

Juanita began to tell Ki about her village, but he found he could not concentrate on her words, for he kept thinking about the possibility of leading those who followed to a great victory.

"Ki?"

He broke away from his troubled thoughts and realized that the senorita must have been addressing him. "What did you say?"

She forced a smile. *"Now* who is falling asleep in the saddle?"

"I was," the samurai confessed. "What did you ask me?"

"I wanted you to tell me about your own village."

"I was raised in Japan."

"I know. Gloria told me you were a samurai. Tell me about this Japan far across the sea."

So to pass the time and to keep their minds off those who kept inching closer and closer, Ki told the girl and the ranch foreman about his childhood and about the country he had left behind with little in his heart but bitterness for the way they treated a child of mixed blood. "Had it not been for Hirata, the old *ronin* who taught me the ways of the samurai, I would have starved to death."

The Mexican girl shivered. "In Candelaria, no child would starve. Not even if he were the bastard son of a murdering Comanche or Apache."

"That is good," Ki said. "I think I would like to see your village someday."

"Oh," she said, "you will! Is that not where you are taking me?"

"To Mexico!" Ed exclaimed. "Señorita, we are going to our ranch before we worry about getting you home."

"No," the samurai said, making a critical decision without further equivocation. "That would be the worst thing we can do. We must reach Fort Wedman."

"But that's in New Mexico territory!"

"Yes," Ki said. "And at least a hundred and fifty miles closer. It's Juanita's only chance, Ed. And even then, I'm not sure we can make it. We may have already ridden too far south."

Ed shook his head. "I dunno about this."

"Trust me," Ki said. "It would be a mistake to lead these men to Circle Star when we have so few hands waiting. Fort Wedman is our only chance."

Ed was not a man to make his mind up quickly, but within five minutes he said, "You're right, Ki. I should have seen the truth of it myself. And I don't think we've come too far south yet. I reckon we ought to swing east just beyond those low hills."

"How far do you think it is?" Juanita asked.

"About a hundred miles is all," Ed told her.

Ki's powerful hands clenched with frustration. The Mexican señorita would not last even a hundred more miles on horseback, and his samurai's code of honor would not allow him to abandon her. For that matter, Ed Wright's cowboy code wouldn't allow it either. So what could they do?

He thought about that all through the second day while the Indians gained ground and Juanita began to fall off her horse. Finally, at sunset, Ki called a halt. He dismounted and tightened the palomino's cinch.

"What are you doing?" Ed asked.

"Changing to a fresher and faster horse," Ki said.

"I can see that. But why?"

"I've got to lead them off," Ki said. "Or at least slow them down."

"You can't do that without getting yourself killed."

Ki looked right at the Texan. "In the night," he said, "not even a Comanche is the equal of a *ninja*."

"But . . . but there's a big bunch of them!"

"I know," Ki said, looking up at the señorita, who was dumb with pain and fatigue, "but I don't intend to kill them all. Only slow and then divert them for the night."

Juanita roused herself. "You're doing this for me." It was not a statement but a fact.

"And for myself and the Circle Star ranch," the samurai told her. "You must ride double with Ed. I will bind the two of you together so that you can sleep through this night."

Ed blinked. "Now why the hell didn't I think of that!"

Ki shrugged. How could you tell a cowboy that he should not feel too badly because he was not a samurai?

It was done in less than five minutes, though they remained long enough to water the horses again. When Ki saddled the palomino and turned away, there were tears in the pretty señorita's eyes. "I will be back," he promised. "For you and for Jessie."

Darkness was falling across the land, and it was welcomed by the samurai as he set Jessie's horse into an easy gallop. It would be another long night, but hopefully more interesting than the last.

# Chapter 12

Ki had no illusions as to what he faced. The Comanche were arguably the finest horsemen in the western world. True, Sun could be expected to outrun anything they owned, but their ponies were accustomed to battle and Sun was not. The palomino was a racehorse, pure and simple. It was deep-chested, and possessed both speed and endurance; but if Ki was forced to close with those who pursued him, Sun's advantages would be nullified.

Ki knew that if he were to have any chance at all of delaying and confusing those who followed, he had to use all his fighting skills as well as his intelligence. And for that reason he decided that his best hope was in attacking the Comanche and Comancheros from behind and trying to kill or disable as many as possible, one by one. So when he came to a deep arroyo, he reined the palomino in to it and rode until he knew that he could not be seen. He dismounted, removed his shirt, and ripped off the bottoms of his trouser legs in the hopes that he would look like a Comanche, with his long, black hair and braided leather hairband.

Ki had his bow and arrows, but there was one weapon that he had not yet used—the *nunchaku*. Ki pulled them

145

out of his pocket and inspected them carefully. They consisted of a pair of sticks attached together at one end by a few inches of braided horsehair. Ki kept many pairs of *nunchaku* back at Circle Star, and the traditional size was long enough to reach from his elbow to the palm of his hand. But the ones he now carried were only half that long—about seven inches. And yet they were a formidable weapon when used by a martial-arts master. These were called *han-kei,* or "half-sized version," and were flat on the inside so that they fit smoothly together. The *han-kei* version were extremely easy to carry because of their shorter size, which is why the samurai preferred them. But like their larger cousins, the *han-kei* could be used to perform virtually every *te* block and strike, and they offered the great advantage of doing so with all the extra power and force of the longer sticks. By holding one stick and whirling the other at the end of its horsehair braid, Ki could generate a tremendous centrifugal force, easily enough to smash an enemy's bones or crush his skull. The *nunchaku,* no matter what size, could also be used like a pair of nutcrackers; a finger, wrist, or other joint caught between the two sticks would crack like a pecan. Ki knew that he might very well be called upon to use the *han-kei*, so he made a few practice swings as the Comanche and Comanchero hunters swept past the arroyo on their mission of death.

Satisfied, he remounted the palomino and raced after the large band of Comancheros and Indians. The dust was heavy, and he had no trouble at all coming up behind them. These men did not expect a lone rider to attack them from behind, and Ki was determined that he would use surprise as his main weapon in addition to the *nunchaku*.

As with any band of men, there were leaders and followers and a few who lagged far behind. It was these men that Ki fixed his attention upon. The last rider of the band was a Comanchero, a large man on a horse that was too old and slow for such a long, brutal chase. Ki edged the palomino in next to him, and when the Comanchero glanced sideways, the wooden *nunchaku* struck him solidly across the forehead. The Comanchero rolled off his horse and vanished in the dust.

Ki moved up to the next man and, raising his hand, he began to whirl the *nunchaku*. When the rider glanced sideways expecting to see the heavyset Comanchero, he was surprised to see the samurai. Before he could react, the *nunchaku* caught him below the ear. His hands flew upward, and then he flipped over backward and hit the dirt and rolled to a standstill. Ki took out three more laggard Comancheros until he overtook his first Comanche. The Indian was struggling and so was his horse, and when the palomino came up to match the Comanche pony stride for stride, the Indian began to whip his weary mount with his bow, still not aware of the samurai.

Once again Ki whirled the *nunchaku*, but the Indian's reactions were sharp and he instinctively flattened on his running pony's neck just as the wooden handle flashed over his head. The Comanche started to bellow out a warning, but Ki drove the ends of the *nunchaku* into the small of his back and the warrior's cry died in his throat. Ki lashed out with a *tegatana* blow and it caught the man squarely in the chest and unhorsed him. Unfortunately, the Comanche pony, now suddenly freed of its burden, burst forward and passed several riders. When they saw the riderless animal, they knew something was wrong, and they twisted around on their horses. One of the men was a Comanchero, and when he saw Ki, he reached for his pistol. Ki's hand darted into his vest pocket and hurled a *shuriken* blade which struck the Comanchero in the side and doubled him up with a pain so violent that he lost his reins and his horse went plunging into the brush.

But the Comanche were better fighters, and they set up a howl that turned the entire band around on their horses. If it had not been dark and dusty, Ki would have been riddled with bullets before he could rein the palomino off their trail and strike out across the sagebrush. As it was, he seemed to be engulfed in a swarm of bullets. The samurai stayed low on his horse's back and let it pick and choose its path of escape.

The men behind him were infuriated beyond reason. Never in their lives had anyone dared to attack them from behind. They could see the many riderless horses, and it told them that a vastly outnumbered enemy had humiliated them. The renegade Comanche were certain that the bare-chested rider who now fled before them was a Kiowa brave out to count *coup,* and that he was with other Kiowa, obscured by the dust, but certainly just ahead. They were determined to run him down and kill him with great respect. Ki had unhorsed all but five of the Comancheros— the ones who had been riding in front. These men, unsure of what was happening, had no choice but to race after the Indians. But after a furious chase covering almost seven miles, Ki was forced to ride over a ridge and skylight himself against the moon and the Comancheros then realized they had been misled by a decoy.

"Hold up!" Daggett cried. "We've been tricked! Let the Comanche take that sonofabitch and let's get the remaining two. Juanita belongs to me first, and then the rest of you can use her for yourselves before I kill her."

The four Comancheros who rode with Daggett grinned with anticipation. Juanita was a fine-looking Mexican girl. Raping her over and over would make this night worthwhile after all. Ki stopped on the ridge-line and twisted in his saddle. The Comanche were coming like a hurricane, but when the samurai saw that the Comancheros were turning back to follow Ed and Juanita, his heart was filled with dread. He knew that he had given the pair an extra fourteen miles, but that might not be enough of an advantage to hold through the rest of the night or until he could somehow shake the Indians on his trail. The very idea of doing that seemed impossible, and yet Ki knew that all things were possible.

He reined Sun so that the palomino would parallel Ed and Juanita on their desperate race to Fort Wedman. Directly in his path lay a range of low mountains, and Ki decided that he had no choice but to sweep wide to his left around them. Doing so would mean that, for the next twenty or thirty miles, Ed and Juanita would be beyond his help or even his sight. Yet what choice did he have? If he stayed to the right, the natural terrain ahead would bring him right back to the Comancheros. They would not allow themselves to be picked off from behind again, and Ki knew that, with Comancheros ahead of him and a swarm of Comanche close behind, he was finished.

There are times in a man's life when he understands very clearly what is the most logical thing to do, and this was one of those times. Even so, it was a difficult moment for the samurai as he reined Sun to the left and set his new course. When the mountains came between Ki and his friends, he had many doubts concerning the wisdom of his choice, but it was too late to change his mind. So he eased his weight higher on Sun's withers and let the tall palomino run as easy as possible in this rough country. The moonlight was strong, and it was Ki's intention to put enough distance between himself and the Comanche that he could rejoin his friends with an insurmountable lead. *If I can do that,* he thought, *then perhaps Ed and I can ambush the remaining Comancheros.*

So it was a horse race, and Ki was on the best animal in West Texas. Jessie had never raced the palomino, but the animal came from racing stock and its speed was renowned. Every fifteen minutes Ki looked back over his shoulder to see that he had widened the gap between himself and the Comanche. He could no longer hear their yells, and they had stopped firing their weapons long ago. The samurai eased up a bit on the palomino, knowing that the mountains that separated him from his friends might run on until daylight.

Hour after hour he raced ahead, extending his lead and growing increasingly worried that the Comancheros might have already overtaken Ed and Juanita. Even worse, the mountain range he skirted seemed to stretch out forever toward New Mexico Territory. The peaks grew taller and the valley that Ki found himself in was climbing. Sun began to labor. Ki reined the horse to a standstill and dismounted. He tossed the reins over the animal's head and began to run with the horse trotting along behind. After the endless hours he had spent in the saddle, Ki rejoiced at the feeling of his blood pounding and his lungs working hard again. He was a man who believed he must keep himself in top physical shape, and now it was paying him dividends.

Daybreak found him still running smoothly. The Comanche were merely a dusty dot far back on his trail. Ki topped a long bench and came to a halt. His chest was rising and falling more rapidly than normal, and there was a sheen of perspiration across his face because of his long exertions, but he was not out of breath.

The land dropped away before him, and far to the west he saw a ribbon of water glistening like a silver thread. "It's the Pecos River," he said with a smile of relief. "And Fort Wedman is up near the headwaters of the Pecos."

Satisfied that the Comanche were no longer a threat, Ki swung onto Sun's back and galloped on. The mountains that had separated himself and Ed Wright were falling away, and Ki said a quick prayer that Ed had been able to keep ahead of the Comancheros.

Less than ten miles from the river, Ki knew that his prayers had not been answered. He came across the tracks of racing horses, and he dismounted and studied them closely. There were better trackers than Ki, but they were hard to find outside of the Apache, who excelled at that art. However, these tracks did not require much expertise. It was easy to read the fact that Ed and the señorita had passed with the Comancheros right on their heels. All of the horses had been running hard, and their trail was going straight for the Pecos.

Ki swung onto the palomino, knowing that he would not spare the horse for these last critical miles. He gave the palomino its head, even as he heard the first scattered rifle-fire along the Pecos. The samurai reached over his shoulder and brought his bow and "Death Song" arrow to his chest. He nocked the arrow, knowing he could do nothing more than hope that Ed had managed to get across the river before the five Comancheros had overtaken him and Juanita.

Their backs were to the river, and there would be no more running. Ed and the Mexican girl had found a thick stand of cottonwood trees, and had taken cover as the Comancheros had opened fire. Ed had intended to cross the river and use it as a barrier, knowing that the Comancheros could cross that stretch of water no faster than a horse could swim. Ed could have picked a few of the leaders off before the others realized they were sitting ducks and retreated to ride up or down the bank and cross beyond his rifle fire.

But that plan went out the window the moment he realized that he and the girl would be the ones shot out of their saddles in mid-stream. So he'd taken cover and opened fire. They had plenty of rifles and ammunition, and maybe they could hold the Comancheros off until Ki arrived.

151

Ed drilled one Comanchero before the others separated into two pairs and dashed into the trees both up and down river of him.

"They got us in a squeeze now," he said grimly.

Juanita was no longer tired. All the grinding weariness had gone right out of her the moment she saw Daggett leading the Comancheros. Daggett, with his lean, whippish body, who had used and abused her own so many hours of the night and day back in Comanchero Canyon. Daggett, who, in a rage, had beaten his previous slave woman to death with his fists, and who might be inclined to do the same to her—after committing unimaginable horrors to her battered and exhausted body.

Grabbing a rifle, the Mexican girl ducked behind a fallen log and gripped her rifle tightly. "You watch that way and I will watch this. I know these men. Don't let them take us alive, Señor. Better to fight and die than face what they would do."

Ed nodded. "It's lucky we got caught in the morning instead of the evening," he said. "They got to come to us, and that isn't something they'll like very much."

Ed saw a Comanchero leap out from behind a tree and sprint closer. Ed snapped off a shot. When he did, two more Comancheros almost hit him with their fire. Splinters of cottonwood filled the air and Ed ducked low. "Them bastards are good shots!" he swore.

"Fighting and killing is their business," Juanita said.

"Here they come!"

The Comancheros came in short sprints. First from upriver, then from down. And the very trees that afforded Ed and the girl protection also protected their advance. A bullet creased Ed's shoulder, and a splinter of wood embedded itself in Juanita's forearm.

"You all right?" the Circle Star foreman asked, trying to hide his deep worry.

The girl nodded. "They are good, no?"

"Damn good!" Ed grunted as the Comancheros again began to charge forward, darting from tree to tree while others of them unleashed a murderous covering volley.

Juanita fired and, much to her astonishment, saw one of them go down.

"You got him!" Ed cried. "Nice shot! That leaves three." Ed twisted back and forth in near panic. "Where's the one that was leading?"

Juanita ducked her head as a volley chewed at the fallen tree. "I don't know," she confessed. "And Daggett is the most dangerous of all."

They only had to wait another five anxious minutes to get their answer. With their backs exposed to the river, they had not expected Daggett to remount and ride upriver, then swim his mount across the Pecos. Now, positioned on the far side, he had a clear though difficult shot across the bright stretch of fast-moving water.

Daggett knew that hitting an object separated by an expanse of water was tricky. There was something about the water that drew a man's eyes down and had a tendency to make him shoot low. So he compensated and aimed for Ed Wright's head, expecting his bullet to bury itself between the man's shoulder blades, or at least the small of his back.

But he overcompensated, and his first bullet only clipped Ed's neck and sent him diving into the brush, yelling, "Get down, Juanita! They got us boxed."

As if in answer, bullets started coming from all three corners of the triangle of death they were now trapped in. It was impossible to cover three sides, and yet they tried desperately to keep the two Comancheros from moving in on them.

The pair were so intent on their cornered quarry that neither man saw the palomino, and the river was too loud in their ears to have heard Sun's drumming hoofbeats. Ki threw himself off the horse's back and froze in his bow-man's stance. The bow in his hand bent, and he seemed not even to aim as he unleashed "Death Song." The arrow swept, cleanly and flat, through the maze of trees, and its whine intensified to the level where it was louder than the Pecos. The Comanchero turned at the sound and stared. He could not see the arrow, but only the samurai who fired it. He raised his gun. That was when the shrill cry of the arrowhead became like the angry shriek of an eagle. The man felt something drive into his chest, and he staggered back against a tree, where the arrow pinned him like a bug to a board.

"It's Ki!" Ed shouted, even as the samurai spun on his heel and reached into his quiver for another arrow.

The second Comanchero was staring at his dead companion pinioned to a cottonwood tree. Too late he pulled himself away from that vision and vainly attempted to raise his rifle and kill the samurai. A bullet from Ed's rifle hit him at almost the precise moment that Ki's second arrow struck him in the chest and sent him backpeddling crazily toward the Pecos. The man struck the water with a tremendous splash and rolled over to float away face down.

Daggett could not see the samurai, but when both of his men died with arrows protruding from their chests, he knew that something was very, very wrong. He was a brave man, but no fool. The arrows meant that they were being attacked by Indians—maybe even Comanche, but more likely raiding Kiowa. Daggett did not care which. He had no intention of being similarly skewered by an arrow shot from the bow of an unseen warrior. Besides, Juanita and the cowboy would die, probably after being tortured and scalped.

Daggett raced to his horse hidden in the trees and threw himself into the saddle. He was getting the hell out of this country and back to Comanchero Canyon where the odds were again in his favor. That Mexican bitch had gotten her just rewards, and that was all that had brought him this far anyway.

# Chapter 13

Ki, Ed, and Juanita wasted no time in getting back into the saddle and heading out of the trees. "We'll swim the Pecos and head upriver along the west bank," the samurai told them.

"Isn't Ford Wedman on *this* side of the river?" Ed asked.

"Yes," Ki said, "but so is the band of Comanche hard on my backtrail."

Both Ed and Juanita spun around and looked back. Sure enough, not more than three miles behind them, they saw the Comanche coming at a dead run.

Ed shook his head. "The fun just never ends in this part of the country, does it."

"Let's ride," Ki told them. "Ford Wedman is going to have a more interesting day than they could even imagine."

Juanita had to force herself to climb back onto the saddle. The insides of her slim legs were so raw that they bled. Ki saw her bite back the pain, and he admired how she tried to look away so that neither he nor Ed saw the tears in her eyes.

Ki rode over to her side. "You are very brave," he told

her. "I wish there was some other way to get out of this, but there just isn't."

"I know, Señor Ki," she replied, trying to smile. "I am no stranger to pain and suffering. I come from a poor family. All my life has been a struggle."

"If it hadn't been," Ki said, "maybe you wouldn't have such great courage right now."

She smiled. "Perhaps. If we get to the fort, will you protect me?"

"From what?"

"From the soldiers," she said. "Soldiers come to my village many times, and they take the girls and... sometimes, they do terrible things to them."

"These are United States Army soldiers," Ki told her. "They're tough and they certainly aren't saints, but they know they'd face a court-martial if they harmed you. You'll be safe."

"I owe you my life," Juanita said. "Somehow, I want to repay you."

Ed Wright shouted, "If we don't get the hell across that river—and fast—there won't any of us be alive to repay anything!"

"He's right," Ki said, reining Sun into the Pecos and feeling the animal wade deeper and deeper until it began to swim.

They crossed the Pecos without difficulty, and when they splashed up on the other side, they took off running. Ki had no idea exactly how far Fort Wedman was up ahead, but from the way that the Comanche were coming and from the agony reflected on Juanita's pretty face, he hoped that it was close.

The Comanche knew this land, and they knew that the river between their quarry and Fort Wedman made a wide bend. Pale Horse understood that the three he followed would be trying to reach the safety of the army fort, and that they would succeed unless he left the river and made a shortcut across the bend. He let out a yelp and selected five of his best warriors on the fastest horses to strike out across the shortcut that would deliver them upriver. So as not to warn those he chased, he shouted for the remainder of his war party to stay after their quarry.

Across the sagebrush he swept, a murderous grin on his face because he was certain that he and his best warriors would intercept the slave girl and the two white men who had stolen her from Comanchero Canyon. But there was more to this even than honor and pride. If these three reached Fort Wedman and were not killed, they would tell others of the great canyon to the north where Pale Horse and his renegade Indians and the Comancheros lived and kept their stolen women, horses, money, and cattle. Pale Horse knew, therefore, that he must stop these three at any cost.

Ki looked back and knew at once that he had lost five Indians and that one of them was the leader, a man riding a tall black horse. "Something is wrong!" he shouted to Ed Wright. "Five Indians have disappeared, and the only explanation is that they know of a shortcut to the fort."

Ed twisted around in his saddle. "There still looks like one hell of a big bunch of them to me! Are you sure?"

"Yes!"

"Well, what can we do about it?"

Ki tightened up a little on the reins. "There's nothing we can do," he said, "except watch out for an ambush up ahead."

Ed swore out loud. "If I ever get back to Circle Star, I don't know as how I'll ever leave it again—even if Miss Starbuck demotes me to cook or stablehand!"

Ki smiled thinly. He glanced at Juanita, and it was obvious that she was in so much pain that it took all her concentration just to stay on her running horse.

They raced on and on, not flat-out enough to kill their horses, but realizing full well that they could not afford to simply lope them nice and easy. The animals were breathing hard; even Sun was showing signs of faltering. The palomino had been ridden as hard as it had ever been ridden across bad land.

"Hey!" Ed yelled, "There's Fort Wedman!"

They had rounded a low hill and had a good view upriver for miles. The fort looked tiny against the backdrop of thousands of square miles of sage and rock. But Ki could see a small flag fluttering in the wind, and he smiled when he glanced aside to see real hope finally spring into Juanita's pain-wracked eyes. "Not much farther," the samurai yelled to her.

The reins were clenched in one hand, and she gripped the saddlehorn with the other. There was so much determination to the set of her face that Ki stared for a minute in wonder. This was a fine woman, all right. One that any man would would be proud to marry and care for.

"Uh-oh!" Ed shouted in warning. "There are those five Comanche you was worried about, Ki! And the bastards are gonna cut us off!"

It was true. The tall Indian on the black horse was already driving his mount towards the Pecos River just up ahead. Ki figured he was less than six or seven miles from Fort Wedman, but it might as well have been six or seven hundred miles for all the help the army could give them right now.

Ki only had two arrows left, and that would not be enough, so he grabbed one of several extra rifles that Ed had packed on the horses and shoved it at the Mexican girl. "Here, tie your reins together and take this."

"But I couldn't hit anything!" she protested. "I would waste the bullets, Señor Ki!"

"Don't worry about wasting anything," the samurai told her.

The girl tied her reins and took a rifle on the run. Ki was not even sure she knew how to work the rifle, but he trusted she had been around the Comancheros long enough to learn. They might just need every bit of firepower they could muster, and if the señorita managed to get off even a few rounds, it might make the difference.

Ed understood as well. He watched the martial-arts master grab a second rifle, and he yelled, "I thought you didn't like our modern weapons, samurai!"

"I don't. But I'm low on arrows and *shuriken* blades, and this will have to do. We've got to hit them before they've swum across the Pecos."

"I don't think we can reach them in time!"

Ki figured Ed was wrong. He levered a shell into the breech of the rifle and gave the palomino a whack across its sweaty rump. Sun responded with a surge of speed that left Ed and the señorita in his dust. The tall palomino flattened out and streaked along the river's west bank so fast that the hot wind made Ki's eyes tear. And Sun brought the samurai within rifle range of the five Comanche before they reached the deepest part of the Pecos River.

Ki bailed off the racing horse. His feet struck the earth and he rolled, hanging on tight to his rifle. When he came to a stop, he knelt and propped his left elbow on his left knee for support. He took aim and fired in one smooth motion.

Pale Horse had not believed that any animal could run like that palomino, and when he saw Ki throw himself from the horse and roll like a wheel only to come to a firing position within rifle range, Pale Horse had a premonition of his own death. He threw himself off the black and dove into the swift water and stayed under it until he reached the bank and cover.

The four other warriors did not react as prudently. Ki shot two of them before the other pair jumped into the river. Ki let them swim to safety, knowing that their weapons were wet and useless.

The samurai raced over to the palomino and remounted just as Ed and Juanita caught up with him. And with the rest of the Comanche's howls of anger growing louder in their ears, they galloped on until the guard patrolling the gate saw them. It must have been quite a picture, the three of them racing for their lives with about twenty Comanche pouring after them like a pack of howling wolves. The stockage gates swung open just enough for them to squeeze their running horses through. The big gates were immediately slammed shut behind them, and the very first impression Ki had was of total chaos. Men were running for the stockade walls, and orders were flying in a seemingly haphazard manner. One look around told Ki that Fort Wedman was in a sad state of affairs. The men looked underfed and sloppy as they scrambled up atop the stockade walls and opened a ragged line of fire, even though the Comanche could not yet have been in rifle range.

An officer with major's stripes came charging out of a cabin. He was fat and slovenly with a dirty blue tunic and scuffed boots. His face was pale and he seemed almost on the verge of panic when he yelled, "Lieutenant Miller!"

A young officer dashed up. The man appeared to be fresh out of military school and could not have been over nineteen, but there was about him a certain amount of control; none of the major's fear was reflected in his young face. "Yes sir!"

"How many heathens are attacking us?"

"About twenty, sir. Hardly enough to—"

"I'll be the one who decides how many constitutes a threat. Are they armed with rifles?"

"Yes sir, but I've ordered Company A to mount up at once and prepare to—"

"You've ordered the men to go out and charge?"

It was clear that the lieutenant had. Even now, men were saddling horses and preparing to form a column. "Yes sir! I thought—"

"Never mind what you thought!" the major screamed. *"I'm* in charge here, not you, Lieutenant. And I say we haven't enough soldiers to counter this full-scale Indian offensive!"

"But, sir, we outnumber them and I know my soldiers can—"

"Attention!" the major screamed at the top of his voice.

Lieutenant Miller came to attention as both Ki and Ed dismounted and scrambled up to see that the Comanche had halted well out of range.

"Hold yer fire!" an old sergeant yelled. "You damned bunch of snot-nosed recruits. Hold yer damned fire!"

Ki swung around to see that Lieutenant Miller was still standing at attention while the Major was giving him hell for trying to usurp his command. It angered the samurai, for a counterattack might have finished off the Comanche. Their ponies were worn out from a long chase, while the soldiers' mounts were fresh.

But this was not his business. The samurai studied the inside of the fort and the men with growing concern. These were the soldiers he had expected to accompany him back to Comanchero Canyon and save Jessie, along with the herd. They were supposed to be trained fighting men, but they looked confused and untrained.

The samurai scowled. No matter. If they could not help, he would leave them and return to save Jessie alone if need be. She would be completely recovered from the snakebite by now.

Ki climbed down from the stockade walls. And though he had only been inside Fort Wedman a few minutes, he had the feeling that he wanted to leave it as soon as possible.

"Chinaman, get down here at once!" the major roared. "Sergeant, bring that man to me at once!"

The sergeant, a tough-looking man in his forties, said, "You better get off the wall and go see what that ignorant sonofabitch wants."

Ki nodded, and when he came face to face with the major, he was seething. "I'm not a Chinaman," he said through clenched teeth.

"And you're not in charge here either," the major growled. He swung to face Ed. "Are you the one that brought this Indian trouble to our doorstep?"

Ed flushed with anger. "Major, Ki here has found Comanchero Canyon. It's not more than eighty miles away, and you can make yourself a general by helping us clear it out."

The major wasn't interested in becoming a general. "My orders are to protect this fort, not go endangering the lives of my soldiers."

Ki had heard enough. The commanding officer was incompetent, cowardly, and a complete fool. The samurai knew it was useless to deal with such a man. "Is there a medical officer at this post?"

The major was caught off guard by this unexpected question. "We have a dispensary, but not a doctor, however—"

"Where is the dispensary?"

"*I'll* ask the questions!" the major shouted.

Ki swatted the man as he would an insect. The hard edge of his hand struck the major at the base of his neck, and the man folded at the knees and dropped into the dirt. Ki looked straight into the lieutenant's eyes. *"You* are in command now. Will you help us while you can?"

Lieutenant Miller stared at the samurai, then at the girl. He looked up to the stockade walls and swiftly reached his decision. "Sergeant, sound the bugle call. Let's mount up and prepare for battle." He looked back to Ki. "The dispensary is over there, and you will find it clean and well stocked. If you need assistance—"

"It won't be necessary," Ki said, knowing he would find a good supply of salve for saddlesores on the dispensary's shelves. He led Juanita over to the dispensary and took her inside. It had five beds and it was clean. A corporal, who was probably in charge of the dispensary, said, "Who are you?"

Ki told the man. Juanita showed him her bloodied wrists and shyly indicated that she had more of the same in her private areas. The corporal handed her a jar of salve. "Apply this liberally," he advised. "I'll be outside if you need anything else."

When the door closed behind him, Juanita set the jar of salve down and said, "I'm worried about you, Señor Ki."

Ki smiled. "We've been outnumbered twenty, thirty to one since the beginning. Now *we* outnumber the Comanche, and you're worried?"

"For you."

The samurai shook his head. "I've come too far to die now. I'll be back in just a while. I don't really think the Comanche want to face a larger force than themselves on open ground. They've come to live and think like Comancheros, and they fight best when they have all the advantages."

"Even so . . ."

Ki opened the jar of salve and began to rub it onto her raw and bloodied wrists. He heard the bugles blow again,

164

and then the drum of hooves. They were leaving to fight without him.

Ki raced out of the infirmary in time to see the young lieutenant lead the charge through the gate. He and Ed ran to the gate and watched, but there wasn't much to see. As Ki had predicted, the Comanche had decided to run and fight another day. This was their land, and no bunch of blue-shirted army soldiers were going to catch them, not even on fresh horses.

The samurai turned on his heel and walked back to the infirmary. He entered and closed the door behind him. Juanita smiled and pulled her skirt up to her waist. She extended the jar of salve to Ki. He stared at the dark mass of hair between her legs, and a smile slowly formed on his lips.

"You need some help?"

"I need *your* help," she told him in a seductive voice. "You are going back to Comanchero Canyon without me, and I may never see you again."

Ki understood. This was not the time or the place he would have chosen to make love to the señorita. But she was afraid there might not be another opportunity, and maybe she was right.

He took the jar of salve and slowly applied it to the inside of her red thighs until they were coated. Juanita leaned back on the bed and sighed with pleasure. When the samurai slipped out of his pants, she took the jar of salve and coated his manhood.

"I don't want to hurt your legs," he said as she held him and gently massaged him into an erection.

"You won't," she whispered, laying back and spreading her thighs very wide apart, letting them hang over the side of the bed so that her feet were just touching the floor. "Your hips are much narrower than the back of a horse, though you are hung like a stallion."

Ki laughed. He slammed his hips forward and his thick staff entered Juanita and made her gasp. "Oh, Señor Ki," she whispered, "I have dreamed much about this moment."

Ki leaned forward and unbuttoned the front of her dress; she was wearing no underclothing. He had also dreamed of this moment since seeing her naked at the Comanchero's cabin. His tongue darted for her nipples; they grew hard as her hips began to thrust to his motion. Ki began to suck and nip at her breasts, and she squealed with delight as his hips rotated faster and faster.

Juanita groaned and her feet danced up and down on the hard wooden floor. "Oh . . . Señor Ki!" she called as she began to lose control of her body and her hot womanhood milked him furiously.

Ki came off his feet, and his hips began to pump furiously. It had been too long since he had possessed a woman, and he was more than ready. With powerful thrusts, he quickly brought the brave señorita to the point of shivering ecstasy. When her spine arched and her fingernails raked his bare back, Ki filled her with his hot, spewing seed.

# Chapter 14

Ki and Ed mounted fresh army horses and prepared to leave Fort Wedman less than two hours after they had arrived. Juanita came to stand beside the samurai. She looked up at him and said, "You promise to return?"

"Of course. I have to help Jessie deliver all those longhorn cattle to Santa Fe."

Lieutenant Miller overheard him. "If the army helps you, we get the first chance to buy your Texas beef."

"I'm sure that Miss Starbuck will make you a fine deal in exchange for the help of your soldiers. But what about him?"

Miller looked down at the major, who had still not regained consciousness. "Private Johnson!"

A young soldier being ordered to stay behind and guard the fort and the major said, "Yes, sir!"

Miller thought about it for a moment. "If the major doesn't wake up before dark, grab him by the bootheels and haul him into his quarters for the night. There's a letter on his desk, detailing the charges I have filed with the Secretary of War. I've already sent a copy to Santa Fe to be forwarded to Washington. These men will all back my story up. I've suggested that the major resign. I think he's ready to anyway. Tell him that I am going to earn my general's stripes. He'll understand."

The private nodded. It was easy to see by his expression that he shared the common feeling of outright disdain for the commanding officer. "Yes, sir," the boy said. "The major, he sure ain't much, is he."

"That will be all!" Lieutenant Miller barked. He looked at Ki and Ed. "Gentlemen, you may lead Company A down the path of glory."

Ki studied the men. Apparently, they had been inactive so long that they had nearly forgotten that they were soldiers until news of Comanchero Canyon had swept through the ranks. Now, they were field-ready, and even looked capable of fighting. It was a damn good thing. Even if the Comanche elected not to return but raid first, the Comancheros would still outnumber them by at least three to one.

Ed Wright must have been thinking the same thing as he looked at the cavalrymen who sat their horses in preparation for the campaign that would take them to the famed stronghold of the Comancheros. "I hope these boys of yours can shoot straight," he said. "Because the Comancheros are all crack shots."

Lieutenant Miller nodded. "We might not be spit-and-polish, but then, out here in this godforsaken country, nothing shiny lasts anyway. And yes, my men can shoot, and they *will* stand in the face of battle. Ideally, of course, they prefer the use of the sabre, and close-quarters fighting on horseback."

Ed shook his head. "The Comancheros would cut them down in a storm of bullets before letting them in close. No, Lieutenant, they had better be thinking of firearms, not swords."

"He's right," Ki said.

The lieutenant shrugged. "I am not a stubborn or opinionated man, and I confess this will be my first major battle against the enemy. Therefore, I am willing to listen to any and all suggestions."

Ki nodded with approval to the young officer. "Lieutenant, you definitely have the brains to make a general in the United States Army. Now, if your troops are ready, let's ride!"

Ki did not glance back at the lovely señorita who had given him such pleasure only a short time before. He knew that she would be safe and that he must now direct all his mental energies to the challenge that lay before them. If the Comanche returned to Comanchero Canyon, they would tilt the odds even further against the soldiers. Perhaps even more damaging, their warning could serve to make things more difficult. There might be extra guards placed on the entrance walls, and they would be much more wary than the pair that Ki had shot.

The samurai wondered if Hector Oxman had harmed Jessie or Gloria Morales in any way. He worried about that a good deal, but there was nothing he could do except ride as fast as the army would follow him before he found out.

Besides, Jessie was plenty capable of taking care of herself, and the young Comanchero, Trevor Morgan, might even help to turn the tide in their favor.

Jessie looked out the window toward the Comanchero camp. "You have to go lead them," she told Trevor. "It's clear that they won't be stalled any longer."

Trevor nodded. "That will mean death for some people. You know that, don't you?"

Jessie frowned, and Gloria Morales said, "We could take this canyon while you are away. We could hold off an army."

Trevor shook his head. "No, he said. "The minute they realized that was your plan, they'd come streaming back in here and overrun all of you. It would be a slaughter."

"What choice do we have?" Jessie said. "I think she has hit upon a good idea. Ride out today. When you have been gone a day, think of a reason to return."

"What reason, Jessie?"

"I don't know. Think of something. By then, Gloria and I will have gotten the other women to help us block off the mouth of the canyon."

"And what if the other women are too afraid to help you?" Trevor said. "They might not be as excited about this idea as you both are."

"They're slaves!" Jessie said.

"They're also alive," Trevor argued. "You don't know what they have been forced to do in order just to stay alive."

Gloria Morales interrupted. *"I* know what they have had to do. Every woman in this canyon has been whipped and beaten. Every Comanchero slave knows that the day will come when she will be traded to the Comanche, where they will be whipped and spat upon by the squaws. They know that they will die within two or three years of that. I say that they will fight if they believe they have any chance at all to win."

Jessie swelled up with pride. Gloria's eyes were flashing, and she had recovered from her bullet-wound to the point where she could move about without great difficulty. She was still weak, but she was a fighter. "Will you be the one who will talk to them?" Jessie asked. "They'll listen to you before they will me."

Gloria nodded, because it was true. Most of the Comanchero slave women were Mexicans. "All right," she said simply.

But Trevor was worried. "I guess we have no choice. I either go with the Comancheros and try to bring them back before they attack some village or settlement, or else they

170

ride without me and be twice as bloody. We can't wait any longer for the samurai to bring the army."

"He's coming back now," Jessie said. "I can feel it inside. He's never disappointed me yet."

Trevor sighed. "All right. But if the Comanche ran him and Juanita down and killed them before they could reach help, I don't think I have much of a chance of saving your hides if this whole thing fails."

Gloria did not believe it. "They might beat us half to death, but they would not kill us. Their needs are too . . . too strong. If you pretended to be angry, we could get away with a whipping."

"I don't think I could let Ross whip either of you with that damned blacksnake of his. Don't forget, I know what it can do to one's flesh. What about the Comanche squaws? Do you think they'll stay out of the fight?"

"We can tell them that we are being attacked by an enemy," Jessie said. "They're at the far end of the canyon. They'll hear the gunfire and prepare their own camp for attack."

"All right," Trevor said, looking at both of them. "You've got an answer for everything, but somehow . . . well, plans go astray."

"We'll unite and block the entrance," Jessie said. "Give us twenty-four hours and then think of an excuse to come back."

Trevor nodded, although he knew there was a very strong likelihood that the Comancheros would kill him before they could be persuaded to return without any slaves or bounty. But he was not going to confide this to the women. So he tied on his gun and selected a good rifle and plenty of ammunition. He went to Gloria Morales and kissed her full on the mouth.

She seemed shocked at first, and even made a pretense of struggle, but Jessie had a feeling she liked it. When

Trevor came to her next, Jessie stepped back and extended her hand. "Good luck," she told him.

The Comanchero leader looked deep into her eyes, and Jessie could see his desire. But that was over now. She was glad that they had made love before, but it was past. And any debt she felt to him was paid. Besides, he really loved Gloria.

"Thanks," he said dryly before he turned and left.

The minute the Comancheros rode through the entrance, Jessie and Gloria called the slave women into the center of the camp. Jessie brought Gloria a chair and made her sit before speaking.

There were about thirty women and they were young, though hard-used, angry, and suspicious. Gloria Morales raised her head high and said, "Some of you know how I was shot trying to escape. Well, what you don't know is that Juanita and the man who took her away is coming back with help to free us."

"How do you know this to be true?" a Mexican woman demanded.

Gloria had anticipated that first question, and she had a very convincing answer. "If they had been caught, the Comanche leader Pale Horse and his braves would have already returned with their scalps."

It was true. Even the woman who had raised the question nodded with agreement.

Gloria continued. "The Comancheros have gone for a day, but they will be back, mean and angry. They will beat us and whip us and all the other things that women do not want to talk about, even to their friends. We must stop them."

"How?" said another woman.

"They have left guns and ammunition here. We can

172

block the mouth of the canyon and keep them out until the samurai returns with help."

The slave women were stunned by the brazen idea, and most began shaking their heads violently. Some, so terrorized by the Comancheros that they could not conceive of ever being free again, began to wail and beat their breasts.

"Stop it!" Jessie shouted at them. "We must do this. You must help us fight the Comancheros."

"No!" a white woman with dull, lifeless eyes screamed. "They will torture and kill us for sure."

Jessie slammed her hand down on the gun she now carried on her hip. She had tried to ask these women to volunteer in this gamble for freedom and life, but now she realized that she would have to force them into action. "We have plenty of guns. Gloria and I are going to block the canyon, and then we will fight. If you don't help and we are killed, the Comancheros will still think you helped, and you will come to no good despite all your cowardice. So you have no choice."

And then Jessie turned and went for a horse and wagon. She would start hauling things into the mouth of Comanchero Canyon—anything and everything that would slow the charge of the men when they returned.

Gloria touched her arm. "I still have one good arm to help you lift things."

"No," Jessie said. "You might reopen the shoulder wound."

Gloria replied, "Then I will get a rifle and come with you. My father knew how to shoot straight, and he taught me as well. I can lift a rifle, Miss Starbuck, and when the fighting begins, I can also pull its trigger."

The perspiration had soaked Jessie's blouse, and her hands were raw from hauling rough pine furniture out of the Comancheros' cabins. She had managed to find a pair of draft animals, and had hitched them up and dragged fallen logs into the entrance as well. It was about then that the other Comanchero women realized that there really was no choice. Either way they were going to be blamed for this, and they might as well at least attempt to put up a fight.

"Look!" Gloria cried with happiness when the Comanchero women came marching up from the camp carrying guns, rifles, axes, and more furniture. "I told you they were fighters. And I'll bet you anything that some of them are crack shots who had to hunt to keep their families from starving."

Jessie could well believe it. These women were from farms and villages, not cities or even towns. They were tough and self-reliant, and they knew how to make do with little or nothing.

Jessie didn't have to tell the Comanchero women anything as they strained and worked late into the night. They were strong, and their hands were already callused from chopping wood for their masters. They set upon the logs Jessie had hauled and cut them into manageable lengths, which they then used to erect barricades and fortifications. It was brutal work, but as the hours passed and the night fell, the air cooled and everyone's spirits lifted.

You could almost feel the growing belief in them that they *did* have a fighting chance. Two women volunteered to go up into the guard-cave on the mountainside, and Jessie made sure that they were excellent shots. Other women joined together to drag every last wagon to the entrance before chopping the axles in two and making the vehicles immovable.

"Just in case," Jessie said, "I want everything doused in kerosene. If it looks as if they are coming through, then we may have to fire everything. We'll allow a few in and cut them down."

The women nodded with understanding and worked

174

even harder. None of them expected to be alive more than a few hours after the Comancheros returned. But at least Hector Oxman was dead, and maybe Daggett as well, and they were the toughest and smartest of the lot.

By midnight they were finished. There was nothing left to do. It was in God's hands now, and many of the Mexican women counted their rosaries.

Listening to them, seeing their bowed heads, Jessie felt weak with the thought that she might have asked too much of a sacrifice. And if Ki was dead, or had not been able to bring help...even if it came but too late...then their blood would be on her hands.

Gloria Morales must have felt the same doubts, because she said, "If we have done wrong, it is with the best of intentions. What good is life when it is not free?"

Jessie nodded, for the words were true. And she knew that, if the Comancheros broke through their barriers and survived the fire, then she would die before she allowed herself to be taken alive. And looking at the women who had trusted her enough to place their lives in her hands, Jessie had never felt more humbled by the awesome responsibility of her actions. Not when she had made million-dollar financial decisions, or even economic ones that might affect the stability of a new ruler's democratic government in some distant part of the world.

"Try to get some sleep," she told the women. "And try not to think about tomorrow."

★

# Chapter 15

Trevor Morgan rode at the head of the Comancheros, just as his father had ten years before. It was strange, this feeling of déjà vu, father and son. Back then, Trevor had been in his teens and had idolized his father, thought of him almost as a god. But now that he had taken his father's place, Trevor knew that leading the Comancheros on a bloody raid had nothing at all in common with godhood.

He led his men west toward the Pecos River, and every mile that they traveled found Trevor struggling to think of some plausible ruse that would return them to Comanchero Canyon with their blood-lust unsatiated. No Comanchero leader had ever returned to that canyon without slaves, gold, money, or at least a few head of rustled cattle. Trevor was sure that, when he made some tepid excuse to become the first, the men he led would shoot him right off of his horse.

"Rider, coming fast!" Ross said, raising a pair of army field glasses. "Why . . . it's Daggett! I guess he must have caught and killed Juanita. But I can't figure out where the rest of our boys could be."

Trevor felt his insides grow cold. Daggett would challenge him for leadership of the Comancheros. He was dead certain of it as they rode forward to meet the lone rider.

Daggett pulled his heavily lathered horse up before them. "Where the hell do you men think you're going!" he demanded, glaring at Trevor in the lead. "Where's Oxman?"

"Dead," Trevor replied, yanking his gun and laying it across his saddlehorn so that it was pointed in the direction of the Comanchero's belly. "And I've taken his place. You have any problems with that?"

Daggett's face stiffened, but with a sixgun already out and pointed at him, he knew he was in no position to fight. "I might later," he said. "But right now, we got us bigger things to attend to."

"Like what?"

"Like the United States Cavalry. There's a company of them coming to wipe us out."

The Comancheros were not easily rattled, but this piece of news sure grabbed their attention.

"Now hold up!" Daggett said. "We outnumber them and we can outfight them too! I say we get back to the Canyon and prepare a little surprise party." Daggett studied Trevor. "Is that all right with you?"

Trevor could not believe this sudden stroke of good fortune. Here was the excuse that he had been struggling for all day. "Sounds good," he told the gunfighter.

Daggett smiled. "After we settle with the army, you and me, we're going to have a little pow-wow about who should be running things now that Oxman is dead. The fact that your pa once called the orders don't impress me a damn bit, Trevor."

"It didn't impress Oxman either, until the moment I put two bullets through his heart in a fair gunfight." Trevor saw Daggett look to the other Comancheros, and when they remained impassive he knew it was the truth.

Trevor smiled and asked, "What happened to Juanita and the man that took her out of our camp?"

"I killed him real slow," Daggett said without blinking an eyelash. "Juanita begged for mercy, but I gave her to the Comanche. Pale Horse took his pleasure and then his braves were waiting in a line ten deep for what was left of her when I left."

Trevor squeezed the butt of his gun. "Who was the man that took her?" he gritted.

"Wasn't a white man. Was one of Pale Horse's braves that took a shine to Juanita. Hell, you saw the arrow sticking out of Ernie's chest. I guess it was plain for anyone to see."

Trevor struggled to hide his relief. So Daggett and the Comancheros had not overtaken Ki and Juanita! "Where are my other men?"

Irritation flashed across Daggett's long face. "You ask too many damn questions, Morgan. The Comanche and the others are doing a little business on their own. They'll be along."

Daggett was such a smooth liar that if Trevor hadn't known about the samurai this story would have seemed entirely believable.

Daggett studied the gun in Trevor's fist. When he spoke, his voice held a clear warning. "You can't carry it around with four fingers forever, can you?"

Before Trevor could think of a reply, the gunfighter spurred his sweaty horse on past, and the Comancheros followed him east along their fresh backtrail. They would stop and make camp for the night and arrive back at Comanchero Canyon in the morning.

Trevor just hoped that Jessie, Gloria and the Comanchero women were ready and waiting to fight.

"Here they come!" one of the women up on the wall shouted.

Jessie took a deep breath and let it out slowly. "Everyone take their places. They won't be able to see what we've done to block the entrance until they're well within our rifle range. And when that happens, let's shoot as many as we can. But remember, Trevor Morgan is our friend. Don't kill him!"

The Comanchero women understood that. They had seen how Trevor Morgan had risked his life for Gloria Morales, and how he had killed the evil Hector Oxman.

Jessie looked up the canyon toward the Comanche camp. The squaws had been told simply that the canyon might be attacked. She had not told them by whom, and they had not asked. They were ready to fight, however, if anyone got through the canyon's narrow mouth and threatened their camp. Jessie knew that the Comanche squaws would remain close to their tipis and out of the fracas as long as there was no immediate threat to themselves or their belongings.

Jessie studied the Comanchero women and figured they had a damn good chance. One main reason for her optimism was that they had thrown up a barricade that would not come down easily. Another reason was that there had been enough rifles left behind by the Comancheros that every single woman had one presently clenched in her fists. Now they were finally ready for what they were sure would be an all-out assault on the canyon once the Comancheros recovered from the first volley.

Jessie aimed at a Comanchero and felt the beat of her pulse right through her trigger finger. She and Ki had been in a lot of bad fixes before, but this was one she would have to fight without the samurai.

"Steady," she said, even as the thought struck her that there were too many Comancheros to stop. There looked to be a hundred, though she knew there were more likely eighty or ninety—men with the look and smell of death stamped upon every crease of their sun-burned faces. "Steady!"

She waited until the very last possible instant. Then, when Jessie saw the one called Daggett suddenly throw up his arm in warning, she aimed at his narrow chest and squeezed the trigger. Gloria Morales had the same target in mind. So, unfortunately, did many of the other Comanchero women. So many rifle bullets struck the tall, thin gunfighter that he was blasted ten feet out of his saddle by the combined impact of their bullets.

Jessie knew that she had made a mistake by not telling each of the women to pick targets relative to their own positions. But it was too late now as the women unleased a deadly volley into the Comancheros. The gunsmoke became so thick in the narrow mouth of the canyon that it blinded them almost immediately.

One of the guards up on the rock face yelled, "They're coming in! There must be—"

Then she was killed, and her death momentarily froze the women. But when the Comancheros hit the barricades, self-preservation galvanized the women into action. No horse could jump or break its way through the barricade, so the Comancheros threw themselves to the ground and came charging through in a murderous assault that raged with a savage intensity.

The women hated Comancheros! They worked their rifles until the barrels were hot. Men and women died. Jessie and Gloria Morales were everywhere at once, fighting, extolling the Comanchero women not to lose heart, and trying vainly to plug up the holes.

The Comancheros fell back in retreat, but there was no

cause for elation because Jessie was shocked to see that at least a third of the women were dead or wounded. "Get the wounded up in the rocks. Two of you tear dresses into strips for bandages and—"

"They're getting ready to come again!" shouted the last guard they had up on the rock wall.

"How many are left?" Jessie cried.

"Fifty, sixty. I don't know. Too many!"

There was no time to care for the wounded, and Jessie knew that there was no way they could stop a second assault. Gunsmoke was still so thick in the canyon's entrance that it allowed the Comancheros to reach the barricade without being seen. And by now they would know that it was the Comanchero women who had stopped them, and that many had been killed in the first assault.

Jessie pulled wooden matches out of her pockets, and so did the other women. They had discussed this early in the morning, and they knew that the time had come to fire the kerosene-soaked barricades. "Wait until they start their charge!" Jessie yelled.

"Here they come!" the guard shouted as bullets smashed into the rock all around her and drove her back into the cavern.

"Fire it!" Jessie cried.

The Comanchero women struck their matches and tossed them onto the wood. There was a horrible moment when the matches seemed almost to die, but then they took a bite of the broken wagons, furniture, and axed trees, and the flames crackled with excitement as the women fell back to the shallow but solid line of earthen bunkers they had dug in the night.

The Comancheros could not drive their horses near the inferno that quickly enveloped the entire mouth of the canyon, and the women were able to shoot many more before they turned back and vanished in the heavy smoke. Its heat became very intense, while overhead the sun blazed down on them. The women perspired and coughed as the breeze capriciously whipped the smoke upward into a thick cloud that could be seen for many miles.

Jessie reloaded, and the Comanchero women, seeing her, did the same. The fire would continue to burn for several hours, and its smoke would be a signal for help.

And if there was no help, then before darkness the fire would die. And so would the Comanchero women.

Ki pointed upward. "There!" he yelled.

Lieutenant Miller raised his gloved hand and slashed it forward and downward. The heavy plume of smoke was just a few miles away, and he knew exactly what he wanted to do. The son of a West Point general, he had eschewed a prestigious and cushy Washington, D.C. staff position and come west in search of field experience only a month before. Now, with the wind rushing in his face and the feel of a good horse between his legs, he was ready.

Ki and Ed were ready as well. The soldiers had stood up to the long, punishing ride very well, and as they closed the distance to Comanchero Canyon, Ki knew that they would fight hard.

"There they are!" Lieutenant Miller shouted a short while later as they topped a hill. "Sound the bugle charge!"

The bugle blew loud and clear, and they swept down the hill with their army pistols in one hand and sabres in the other. Ki drove his horse into the fray with a vengeance, and he saw Trevor Morgan down on the ground firing up at the Comancheros. Trevor was wounded, but Ki had no time to help the man as the battle raged and swirled.

To their credit, the Comancheros fought gallantly and died well, but they were trapped at the canyon's mouth and caught in a crossfire with no place to run. The man named

Ross tried to kill the samurai, but one of Ki's last arrows found its mark and he died violently.

Ki whirled his mount around just in time to see a soldier drive his horse at the downed Trevor Morgan. The corporal's horse trampled the Comanchero leader. Then the soldier jumped from his mount and charged forward with his sabre.

Trevor Morgan was struggling to raise his head. The samurai ripped the *surushin* from around his waist, spun it overhead twice, and sent it whirling to wrap itself around the corporal's knees, toppling him. The sabre slashed downward but fell short, and before the determined soldier could crawl near Trevor and finish him off, Ki used a sweep kick to send the sabre spinning out of his reach.

"This one is our friend!" Ki shouted.

The man looked up at the samurai and swore with exasperation. "Well, how in the goddamn hell was I supposed to know that?"

But the samurai was beside Trevor and rolling him over. He quickly saw that Trevor had been shot twice, but that neither wound was fatal. The horse which had trampled him had left a nasty scrape on the side of his face.

Ki turned to watch as the last of the Comancheros fell and died. He studied the mouth of the canyon and the great fire that had saved Jessie and the Comanchero women from being slaughtered. "I'm afraid we'll have to wait a few hours to see the women," he told Trevor Morgan.

The last Comanchero smiled up at him. "A few hours? Hell, mister, I been waiting all my life to see the end of Comanchero Canyon!"

Jessie watched Gloria fuss over Trevor Morgan's wounds. Her cattle were fat and would be reluctant to leave, but there was a ready market at Fort Wedman and Santa Fe, and maybe the thousand head she had given to Pale Horse and the renegade Comanchero yesterday to keep and raise for beef would change their lifestyle.

As if reading her mind, Ed Wright said, "You and the lieutenant, you were both pretty generous with Pale Horse after he showed up."

"Generous?"

"Well, yeah. Giving him and his people a small herd of the best Texas longhorn cattle money can buy, not to mention the right to stay in this canyon."

Jessie shook her head. "This is *their* canyon and it's *their* land, not ours. As for the cattle, maybe they really will find that ranching is healthier and even more profitable than raiding. And if they don't, we and the army will always know where to find them."

Ed grinned. "So you and the lieutenant figured you bought yourself a chief."

Jessie watched the soldiers as they began to haze her cattle out of the canyon toward Santa Fe. They were having a rough time with the longhorns. "Ed, be patient with these soldiers. Try and remember that they're not Circle Star cowboys."

Right then, a steer broke back up the canyon for the tall green grass it had gotten accustomed to. Four soldiers turned their horses and chased after it, but none of them had ropes or even saddle horns on their little McClellan saddles.

The steer ran free and the soldiers had to chase the stubborn beast nearly three miles before it quit running for lack of breath. Ed's face revealed his pure disgust, and when he turned to Jessie, he said, "Mistake these jokers for real cowboys—that'll be the day cowboys ride rabbits!"

Then he formed a loop in his lariat and galloped off to rope the steer, because he was the only man in Comanchero Canyon who knew how.

184

Watch for

**LONE STAR AND HICKOK'S GHOST**

seventieth novel in the exciting
LONE STAR
series from Jove

*coming in June!*